JOYPUNKS

ISBN: 979-8-9923914-0-4
LCCN: 2025902827
Independently published by
Bad Trips Literary, LLC
joypunksbook.com

Cover and book design by Lauren Grosskopf

JOYPUNKS

AKA Writing On the Wall

By **FLETCH FLETCHER**

BAD TRIPS LITERARY, LLC

(BTL)

Praise For Joypunks

"A philosophically stimulating novel crackling with emotional liveliness... A thoughtful rumination on human mortality is achieved as well, one that cannily investigates the wages of too much knowledge." - *Kirkus Reviews*

"4.5 Stars Out of 5; Fletch Fletcher's JOYPUNKS is a sharp, gritty novel that examines predetermined mortality through the lens of addiction and friendship. Packed with booze, drugs, and existential dread, it's a wild debut that swings big and lands punches with its bruised-heart energy." - *Indie Reader*

"4 Stars out of 5; A young man struggles to feel bravery and hope in the face of his imminent demise in the satirical speculative novel *Joypunks*." - *Clarion Reviews*

"(Readers) will sympathize with Fletcher's relatable cast, who feel fully realized on the page and communicate their confusion and hopelessness in passionate dialogue that evokes philosophical discussion about how long a life should be to make it meaningful. Fletcher's character development and dialogue shine in this mature effort." - *Booklife.com*

"I've read *Joypunks* (twice, actually) and I can say that if I were still publishing I would ask to publish it... It's unusual and clever, and I think it has a chance of selling well. Best case scenario, it could catch on among the 20-something crowd and emerge as a type of cult novel. I think the premise is very clever, and Fletch seems to work it well." - Jack Estes, founder of Pleasure Boat Studio

Dedicated to my dad who once said
he had an idea for a story,
but didn't know how to write it.
Hope I make you proud.

"I'd rather laugh with the sinners than cry with the saints.

—Billy Joel

"Death is only the end if you think the story is about you.

—*Welcome to NightVale*

"Once we have accepted the story we
cannot escape the story's fate.

—P.L. Travers

"Around my neck hangs superstition, hanging from a chain,
because I got my Gods, but in the end I make my own way.

—*The Cat Empire*

"To fall in love and fall in debt
To alcohol and cigarettes and Mary Jane
To keep me insane
Doing someone else's cocaine
And there's nothing wrong with me
This is how I'm supposed to be
In a land of make believe
That don't believe in me.

—*Green Day*

Prologue

I turn eighteen today. I heard that the brain doesn't actually stop developing until I'm twenty-five. I can now vote, join the army, and buy cigarettes among other things, yet in the eyes of science I suppose I am still a child, still learning and growing. These thoughts were of little interest to me however as I sat in the passenger seat of Luke's car.

I glazed out the window as we drove through suburbia. We had left the highway and we're now coasting through the heart of Flagstaff, Arizona. Pine trees were glistening against the fuzzy skeletons of their leafed counterparts. Spring had just started and the light green of life was returning to our world. People on the street were smiling as if winter was permanently behind us, the cheerful optimism of denial. As if we all didn't know what was awaiting us.

Luke had given up speaking to me at this point. Initially he was trying to reassure me before simply talking to fill the void. Eventually my one word answers led him to simply turning up the volume on the speakers. His anxieties may have been secondhand, although I believe he truly is a better person than that. His parents had taken him when he was on his trip, but I had asked him to take me on mine. It was easier this way for me.

We pulled up to the Department of Designated Dates around noon. It was a large two-storied building and, like any government building, its exterior held all the charm of a slab of concrete. Luke was avoiding eye contact with me for most of the ride. I was just focusing on deep breaths and mindlessly scrolling through Twitter on my phone. He parked and we momentarily sat in silence after the music switched off with the car.

"Hey, man, you want me to come with you?

"No, I'm fine, I said as I unbuckled my seat belt, "I'll be okay. I just need to get this over with.

"Alright, just remember you've wanted to do this forever and now's your shot, plus in the long run everything's the same anyways.

"Yeah, thanks. I exited the car and turned around. "Seriously, though, thanks for taking me.

"Yeah, of course, figured this'll be less stressful than riding with your parents, he said with a smirk.

I forced a smile and shut the door before heading toward the front door of the DDD. I was focusing on my breath while trying to ignore the nausea swirling at the bottom of my stomach. Toward the entrance were a man and woman sitting behind a cheap plastic table. A large sign hanging from the table read, "Your fate doesn't define your future, in swirly writing with waterfalls and crap like that in the background. They were both dressed casually as if they were off to a picnic, in T-shirts and jeans, yet they radiated a much more serious energy. I smiled politely and gave a faint wave, hoping they could tell I wasn't interested. Unfortunately, they didn't seem to care.

The man chirped in, "You know ignorance is bliss, oftentimes ...

"Yeah, yeah, thanks. I've heard all the Gnostic stuff. I'm going to go get my numbers right now. Thank you, though.

The man nodded. "Well, happy birthday, and know we'll be praying for you.

I said thanks and kept walking. The door at the entrance was marked very officially with the government seal as I pushed through the door. The lobby had stale air that permeated the room along with all the charm. I walked up to the front desk and approached an older man with a faded button-up.

"Hi, I'm here for my numbers. I don't have an appointment, but I'm okay with waiting.

The man chuckled politely, "We'll send you in with an operator in a second. Don't worry, you'll be fine.

I nodded, took the ticket he gave me, and sat down in cheap, polyester chair in the back. I ignored my phone messages, closed my eyes, and I blasted old rock music through my earbuds. I held my knees with my hands to keep them both from shaking. I don't know who I cared about fooling, but I tried to remain calm.

The room was rather large and all the chairs pointed toward a large TV in the center of the room with numbers of tickets being called. There were two other TVs with sports and some talk show with subtitles on, but I don't think anyone actually cared to watch. The room had a few other people in it; only a few people didn't look like they were sweating bullets.

It was easy to spot who else was celebrating their birthday, a couple of others kids my age (literally) were waiting, a few with their parents or someone else there. I recognized another kid from my high school, but neither of us knew the other enough to say anything. Besides a few supportive whispers here and there, the room was silent like a monastery, except no meditation, just prayers.

One girl a couple seats in front of me actually got up and began pacing in front of her parents. She was holding her mother's hand as she was hyperventilating between sobs. They seemed embarrassed, but too kind to say anything. Nobody cared though, obviously, we all felt that level of panic in us one way or another.

About thirty minutes in, my number popped on the screen and I forced my legs to stand. My breath was patchy as I made my way to the front where a forty-year-old woman was standing behind a barrier and a glass, protective screen. Her seemingly singular unique quality was being the only person in the room with a face of pure indifference. She stared at me blankly as I held my ticket up in front of her. She opened a door and motioned for me to come.

I followed her through a sparsely decorated hallway into a small, side room. The room had two chairs along with a computer on a desk and a first-aid kit hanging on the wall. The far side of the wall featured a large, metal tube jutting out; the tube was empty and dark with hardly any light piercing inside of it. I glanced at it as the doctor pointed to my chair. The machine haunted my peripherals.

"Alright, so before the procedure I am mandated by the government to read you the following statement.

"Yeah, look, I've already heard it. Can I just get out of here?

She smirked with sympathetic eyes. "No I'm afraid not. Can I begin?

I nodded and she did.

"We possess the ability at the Department of Designated Dates to now accurately predict the time of your death due to natural causes. While you are not required to learn your dates, it is highly encouraged for easy access to retirement savings, social planning, and so forth. It should be noted that you can still die from incidents such as car accidents, drug overdoses, murder, and so forth. This option is only offered on a citizen's eighteenth birthday and, after the day has passed, nothing can be reversed. While some choose not to see their dates, studies have proven that they result in the same time of death. Since you are now an adult, all responsibility for this procedure now falls on you. Do you understand and still wish to proceed?

She looked up and I nodded again.

"I need a verbal confirmation.

"Okay …. Yeah, let's do it.

"Okay, please put your hand in the gizmotron.

I slowly pushed my right forearm into the dark, looming hole; the air felt cool on my skin causing goosebumps to ripple down my arm. After I was nearly in shoulder-deep, I twitched my hand back slightly as I grazed an iron bar that gave me a slight shock.

"The bar has a slight electrical charge in order to make it harder to instinctively pull free. We don't want you getting half an answer.

While her tone was cheery, it was clearly meant as a warning. I reached in and grabbed the bar again; I felt the tingle as my fist closed around a cold metal bar.

She counted down to three and pressed a large button on the side of the wall. The hole glowed red and I yelled as the lasers branded their fortune into me. My left hand flew and punched the side of the wall which had clearly been reinforced for such incidents. The nurse had already stepped back, most likely predicting this reaction.

After what felt like the longest minute of my life, the machine shut off and I pulled my hand out from the machine. Seared in black was a date on the inside of my wrist. I heard the doctor gasp unconsciously as I looked at it.

"Well, fuck, I managed to get out with a crack in my voice.

Chapter 1

A couple years of later

I woke up in a hospital bed. My head felt like it was very lightly tapped with a sledgehammer. The artificial light blasting from the ceiling burned my eyes and I went to block it with my hand which only jerked the bed sideways. My peripherals showed my arm strapped to the bed, the reason being immediately understandable as I had a plastic tube going down my throat. I gagged briefly, but it was more at the thought of it as opposed to anything else. My brief struggle must have caused some attention because a nurse came to check in on me. She was about fifty and had a plastic smile.

"Hi. Daniel, right? Okay, last night you overdosed on a mixture of alcohol, cocaine, and MDMA. Our records say that this isn't the first time that you've been with us for this, so I shouldn't need to explain everything that's happening. Hopefully, this we'll be our last visit. Anyways, your doctor will be here to check up on you in just a minute.

I tried getting as comfortable as I could, which is difficult with a tube in your throat, while I closed my eyes to fight the light. In the meantime, I focused on deep breaths and touching my fingers to my thumb in order to try to make some type of repetition.

Okay, so last night I went to the Lumberyard with Naomi and Brian, we were rolling, then we went to the club where Brian knew the bouncer who was, like, named Jason-something. We were drinking and dancing, I think I re-upped in the bathroom with Brian ... and that's about where things get to hazy to follow. Goddamn it, did I really mix Molly and liquor again?

My body made an attempt at a sigh as I tried opening my eyes again to get adjusted to the light and take in the room. Normal hospital room, all the chairs were thankfully empty (no family or inebriated friends), and in the far corner on TV some local reporter was interviewing some dipshits. The clock above the door said it was a little past eleven which means I probably got to the hospital sooner rather than later, which was good. That is, if it's a.m.—if it's p.m., not so good. My focus shifted at the sound of a doorknob as a doctor came in.

He was looking at a clipboard and sat down in a swirly (the chairs that spin) while pulling the chair up to next to me. He placed the clipboard on the table next to me before sighing and glancing at me like an exasperated teacher.

"Look, believe it or not, I understand it. Your numbers aren't great, drugs are fun and all that, but you've still got plenty of time left. If you keep up at this pace, you're gonna end up dying in the streets or a prison cell, neither of which will do anyone any good. We have some programs that could help you get clean or possibly try to help others."

He dropped off a couple of sheets of paper on the table next to me

"We'll pull the tube out in a little bit and you'll probably spend another night here.

I tried saying "another but my voice just came out muffled

He got up and went to leave the room. "Get your shit together.

And with that he left the room. I closed my eyes and tried to go to sleep. No dice.

I was able to determine that it was now two o'clock in the morning because no one turned the TV off. On the plus side, after a lifetime of nonstop bombardment, I can now tell you all about the miracle nonstick pan, as seen on TV. Superglue doesn't even stick to it and you get a lifetime warranty so, at $15.99 plus shipping, it's a steal. Eventually a nurse came in and apologized after turning it off, leaving me drifting in and out of consciousness while I was trapped with my own thoughts.

The first nurse returned in the morning. Apparently the rules are different on your second overdose, the first time I just got a stern talking to. This time I got sent over to the loony bin.

Also they get super mad when you call it the loony bin.

Chapter 2

I was woken up around nine by the same nurse named Cathy. She turned on the TV and said that I would be leaving soon. The TV switched onto a documentary about how different cultures reacted to the numbers. Rwanda banned its citizens from receiving their numbers since they played a crucial role in the Rwandan Genocide. People with low dates were targeted in the riots and mass killings. So now no one could get numbers. Those who wished for them had to denounce their citizenship and move.

In most Middle Eastern countries, those who received numbers under thirty were sent to work camps for "moral failings. This had long been determined to be a crime against humanity by the U.N. and had led to many embargoes. Still the practice persisted. Those who could afford it would leave the country to get their numbers and come back afterward—assuming that their numbers weren't under thirty.

In China, everyone was required to receive their numbers. The government decided that you could only retire when you had one seventh of your life left. In the rare cases where people refused to get their numbers they were often forced to work until they dropped dead. People applying for jobs were required to put their numbers on their résumés. While some fought the morality of this, it was often chalked up to a cultural difference as opposed to a direct violation of human rights.

In Indonesia, anyone who was going to die under forty had a parole officer assigned to them to keep tabs on them.

The list goes on.

Cathy comes in and clicks the TV off. "Enough of that. Time to go.

She gave me my belongings back (briefly); just the things from my pockets: keys, phone, and pepper spray. Seemed kinda unwise to give me a weaponized vegetable when heading to the loony bin, but I figured that the doctors there would take it away from me when I arrived there. On the way to the ambulance I borrowed a Sharpie from the lobby desk and wrote Naomi's number on my wrist for later when my phone was confiscated. I had a few texts from Naomi, Brian, and someone named Alexis (whose messages were followed by a bunch of emojis). I decided I'd call them later when I was feeling better and maybe have remembered Alexis of the emojis.

The ambulance ride was short. I spent most of the time talking to the EMT about what music we liked. I jokingly told him that Owen Vonn was definitely better on Molly and he jokingly agreed, although he didn't seem like the type to look for proof. We pulled up to a small building that looked like it had a courtyard in the middle. They took me through the lobby, which had a couple people waiting, and into a hallway with locked doors. We entered the locked room. Once the doors were locked behind us they unlocked the doors in front of us and let me into the psych ward.

The lobby had a large circular desk in the middle with busy-looking nurses behind it.

Several hallways lined with rooms split off from the hall-way. There was also a laundry room, a meeting room, and a rec room filled with patients. They showed me to my room at the end of the hall and then left me alone.

First thing I did was get a nicotine patch from the nurse cause I definitely needed one.

Luckily they don't want us off all of the drugs in our system. Second thing I did was raid the library. They had a small section of books in the corner of the rec room. They had about five fiction books and dozens of Gnostic and Waterson bibles. I grabbed some sci-fi book called *Spindrift* and made my way to my room. It was a small room with a twin bed and a desk with a chair. The chair was significantly weighted to make it difficult to move or pick up (or hurl at nurses). I curled up in the corner of the bed and started my new book. On the wall behind the pillow a poem was written:

We REBEL against melancholy
We bare our souls open to the world
We JOYPUNKS cursed to die young
We find happiness in the insanity only we truly live.

I thought about the poem as I fell asleep.

* * *

When I woke up I wrote Naomi's number in crayon on a Sudoku puzzle that I took from the rec room. Then I took a shower, threw on my scrubs again, and walked to the pay-phone wall. I dialed Naomi's number and crushed the paper into my pocket for later. A nurse walked over, and after a brief discussion, allowed the call to be placed and then the ringing started.

"Naomi, it's Danny.

"Motherfucker! What took you so long? said Naomi.

"I just got to the psych ward, I called as soon as I could, I lied.

"Well, it felt like forever. We tried calling the hospital and they wouldn't patch us through to you. We were told you were stable though.

"Yeah, well, they had a fucking tube down my throat. I don't think I could've talked anyways.

"God, that sounds terrible.

"Yeah, don't OD, okay?

"I'm not the one ODing left and right, unlike you, know how to handle my dru—wait, is anyone listening on this line?

"What? No, Naomi, be serious. Nobody cares.

"Fine. How long are you gonna be stuck in there?

"Haven't talked to any of the doctors yet, but probably like a week or so. Say do you think you can go to my job and say I'm in the hospital and can't come in to work?

"They'll try calling you.

"Yeah, well they'll have to wait.

"Sure, but they're going to fire you.

"I know, but can you do it anyways?

"Fine … you know you really scared me—

"Look, I'm sorry, I fucked up. I know.

"This is the second time. You cut it really close, you had bile coming out of your mouth and everything.

"Look, I get it, I'm an idiot, but it's only like five years anyways. Who gives a shit?

I could hear Naomi get off the phone, after some background chatter I heard a familiar voice.

"What'd you say to piss off Naomi?

"Just that I'm dead in five years anyways. I could hear him laugh over the phone.

"That's funny, but you better not die early on me. Alright, bro?

"Yeah, yeah, what happened two nights ago?

"You did two points and a third one in the bathroom. Got drunk and then took some chick back to do coke. I left you two alone around five in the morning. She woke us up around eight, screaming.

"Fuck. Was the girl cute?

"Nope, he said laughing. "Fat and wouldn't shut up the entire time. Honestly you had her so coked-up she was talking like a motorboat.

"Fuck me. Alright, hopefully I'll be outta here soon.

"Yeah, you talk to the doctor yet?

"No, not yet.

"Look, just say what they want to hear, take whatever pills they give you, and generally act like a gentleman, and you'_ be out in no time.

"Yeah, I know, I'll be amiable.

"What?

"I'll be agreeable. Is Naomi okay?

"Yeah, she'll be fine. We'll come visit you later, alright?

"Visiting hours are between three and five.

"Sounds great. Your family know?

"Nope, and let's keep it that way.

"Do you think me and your dad talk a lot?

After a little more small talk, I hung up the phone. I took in the lobby slowly. All the nurses were happily typing away behind their computers, updating their files on what kinda neurotics we have, or just playing Minesweeper—I couldn't tell ya. A disheveled-looking woman was staring at me, so I turned around and chose to go into the rec room over my bedroom. Figured, safety in numbers.

Some people were watching a Russell Crowe movie and everyone else was busy drawing. I laid down on the couch and joined in on the movie while keeping my peripherals on the woman. It took about thirty minutes before she approached me.

"You're pretty.

"I promise, you're not interested.

She gave me a slip of paper with her number on it and a heart. I thanked her, and put it in my pocket before going back to the movie. Actually a decent film.

* * *

So the doctors meeting went horribly. I sat there and they told me my dangerous activity suggested I was borderline suicidal. I showed them my numbers and they refused to agree that they had anything to do with anything. They wanted me on a new antidepressant and mood stabilizer. They asked me if I was still taking the antidepressant they prescribed last time. I admitted that I had stopped taking it about a year later. They stressed the importance of sticking with your medication and that's where I started zoning out. Long story short, they wanted to keep me on the drugs long enough that I could feel the effects of them before releasing me. I said okay. Now I was sitting in my room.

Being in the psych ward is like getting sober, it's remarkably boring and sometimes needed. I was not in the mood for either of those two things, yet, here I was. Unlike the movie *One Flew Over the Cuckoo's Nest*, nothing is going on and everyone is surprisingly nice. I thought about trying to convince one of the nurses that I was an alcoholic who would go into shakes to see if I could get prescribed a beer, but I decided against it. Would probably only extend my time in the joint.

The doorknobs in here were all curved and smooth to make it impossible to hang something (or someone) on. It occurred to me if I was really that desperate I could simply smash my forehead into the doorknob until I died of internal hemorrhaging, but my heart wasn't really in it. It also occurred to me that I had really died and I was in Purgatory, but that seemed unlikely. Probably a better idea for a story than anything else.

Around noon, we had lunch, which was decent. Cheeseburgers and baked beans with juice boxes. After that, there was really nothing else to do except watch TV, talk, read, or attend classes. The classes were mostly the same, basically group therapy. I hated admitting that I actually got something out of them, but I did. They talked of an ancient Native American proverb about an evil wolf and a good wolf fighting inside of you. A boy asked which wolf would win and the group leader said the one you feed.

By dinnertime they gave me my clothes back and I changed into them. A little awkward being in rave clothes, but better than scrubs. I was wearing cut up jeans and a Daft Punk tank top.

My best friend in there was a girl named Carly. She was in for "overdosing on Molly.

Basically she had just passed out because of dehydration, but it was probably for the best that she was in there. Probably for the best that I was in here, too.

So with nothing else to do, I opened my book and waited on time passing.

Chapter 3

"We'd feel more comfortable releasing you into the hands of family members. Remember, we advised you to perhaps get a new group of more productive friends.

"So you're saying I have to stay longer unless my family picks me up?

"We just think that reaching out to family would show progress; we'd love to see more effort from you.

"Okay, fine, I said, rolling my eyes when they were out of sight.

My family could be my drug dealers for all they know. I mean they're not, my friends are, but they don't know that.

So with a begrudging apathy, I approached the phone bank and dialed my older sister's number which luckily I had memorized. As the phone rang, I thought briefly of hanging up and spending the extra time here. Probably not worth it.

"Hello? my sister said.

"Hey, Reagan, it's Danny.

"Oh hey, where are you calling from?

"The Coconino Psychiatric Facility, why? There was a long pause over the phone and I banged my head against the wall waiting for her response.

"Are you trying to get clean? she asked.

"Yes.

"Did you check yourself in this time or did you overdose again?

"Is that really that important? I said banging my head against the wall again.

"God-fucking dammit, are we serious right now?

"Look, I'm genuinely trying to get my shit together, okay?

"What do you want?

"Can you pick me up?

"Fine, she replied hanging up.

Could've gone worse, quite frankly.

* * *

Around noon, my sister came into the psych ward. Luckily Naomi had brought me a spare change of clothes so I was no longer dressed in rave gear, just an old hoodie and jeans.

Conversely, my sister was wearing a NAU T-shirt and jeans with her hair in a tight bun. She looked disappointed as I approached; I tried smiling to relieve the tensions. She gave me a quick hug and proceeded to fill out the paperwork up front.

Eventually she finished and we went back into the hallway and waited for the doors to close behind us before the doors in front of us opened. I was carrying my few belongings in a brown paper bag that hung by my feet.

"Let's go.

I grabbed my bag and hurried after her out of the room. Her quick pace made it difficult to keep myself balanced as we strode through the hallway. I used my hand to cover my numbers as I pretended to avoid the stares of the other patients. Although, in hindsight, nobody probably cared; most people in the psych ward don't have the luxury to let their mind wander enough to psychoanalyze other people.

I felt light-headed and nauseous, but decided to keep this information to myself, suspecting that I would get little sympathy from my older sister. I followed her into the parking lot where I got in the passenger seat of my old car.

"So the other night …

"The other night?! she stifled a laugh. "You came in at ten in the morning, dumbass. What do you think happened?

"Well, whatever. Look I fucked up, okay?

"Yup.

"But it won't happen again, alright?

"Uh-huh.

"Honestly.

"You gonna go to rehab this time?

"No, I'll be fine … is dad pushing that shit again?

"Probably will be. I haven't told him yet.

"Oh.

"Yup.

Reagan had pulled into the street at this point, her shoulders were sagging as she kept both hands firmly on the wheel. I plugged my phone into her car and my phone started immediately blasting EDM through her speakers. Reagan clicked the speaker off, returning the car to silence.

"Really, that's what you felt the mood called for? Reagan said without taking her eyes off the road.

"No, that was just the last thing my phone was playing before I went under, I suppose …

"The last thing you nearly heard was that shit?

"I suppose.

Reagan sighed and continued staring down the road.

* * *

We pulled into my (old) house. Typical middle-class American house with the two-car garage and the basketball hoop in the yard. We lived in Flagstaff, Arizona, which despite the state's reputation, looked more like any cookie-cutter suburbia than a John Wayne movie.

Secluded in the mountains, two hours away from Phoenix, and suddenly we became a ski-resort kinda town, just with less rich people and more college kids.

I tugged at the hospital bracelet at my arm until it snapped off. Reagan rolled her eyes as we she stepped out of the car.

"You know, I'm not gonna let you leave without you telling them, she said without turning around.

"Yeah, I know, I said following her up the driveway. "Do you think you could distract them for a second just so I can go upstairs and change real quick? I'd just rather not walk in dressed like a complete asshole.

"Yeah, of course.

She opened the front door and yelled, "Mom! Dad! Danny's here and he's spending the night. Come say hi!

I could hear my mom yelling, "Really? from around the corner. I quietly informed Reagan that she could drop dead, before yelling, "Gotta go to the bathroom upstairs, real quick though!

I hauled ass up the stairs and turned the corner into my room.

Chapter 4

My old room was decorated in posters of old rock bands and a couple of movies I liked in high school. The dresser was covered in childhood photos. The room felt like an empty memorial to the high-school kid who was gonna go out and live the American Dream, write a hit movie, and then go on to change the world.

I itched my arm where they pulled out the IV as I looked in the mirror. I was pale and tired, looking like a vampire on the summer solstice.

I slid on a plain, collared shirt and khaki pants as I hid my former clothes in my backpack.

After briefly checking my backpack for deodorant, I settled with the stick on my desk that dragged across my skin like sandpaper. I grumbled and left my old room behind.

My parents were both cooking in the kitchen with the Diamondbacks playing on the TV as background noise. Reagan was standing in the middle of the kitchen talking to them about something that happened in one of her classes. They looked over as I entered the room.

My mom's smile turned slightly quizzical and my dad immediately looked at Reagan who pretended to be focused on her phone.

"Hey, sorry, guys. Naomi got a promotion yesterday and we all went out for drinks. Then, unfortunately, I made the mistake of promising Reagan that'd I'd be coming over tonight to surprise you guys.

"Well I don't know if I'm surprised, my dad replied before

going back to simmering something.

"So, how have you been? Everything still good? my mom asked.

"You know same old, same old. Job's going fine and all that stuff, I replied as Reagan gave me a bit of a dead stare. "What's for dinner?

* * *

We sat around the table which my sister and I had set. My parents set down the food and we stopped to do prayer. My family was Gnostics which meant they didn't believe in receiving your numbers because they felt it would determine your path, so one was supposed to join the church officially at eighteen after declining your date. While, occasionally, people would rejoin later after receiving their numbers and cover their numbers up, I had no real urge to.

Whatever religious beliefs I was still holding onto before my eighteenth birthday had since drifted far away. I closed my eyes along with my family as we waited, from either politeness or just laziness to argue or both.

No prayer came to me and my thoughts came and went. I waited till I heard my sister open her eyes and begin eating to follow suit. My parents opened their eyes soon after that and we began talking again.

Gnostics were the second largest religion in the US after Watersons, but the aspect of not knowing one's number ended up turning away a decent amount of people. Knowing your numbers helped with a lot of big decisions such as retirement plans or applying for loans which are decent excuses. Curiosity is what killed the cat though, most people just want to know.

The biggest difference between Gnosticm and Waterson was that Gnostics believed that people's numbers ended up defining their lives whether they want them to or not. Watersons believed that the numbers were a reflection of your morality, so if you hit a hundred, God probably thinks you're a saint, more or less. So, if you're gonna die at a young age, essentially you're an asshole in the eyes of God.

Good news is my parents don't think I'm cursed by God, they just think I'm a dumbass with no direction, which is relatively accurate in fairness to them. It's not great, but they're not wrong and plenty of other people have it worse, so ya know.

"So what's the plan? my dad asked.

"For? I replied.

"Life, Danny. What's your plan?

"For what? The next six years? Am I supposed to have some kind of plan?

"Some semblance of one.

I kept pushing my food around. "Look, I'm just trying to enjoy my life and hopefully not ruin anyone else's.

"Sounds impressive.

"What the fuck do you want me to do?

"I don't know, I figured you would maybe try to get your shit together after your OD.

"Hey, can we not mention that right now? my mom chirped in.

"What? He's right, Reagan said.

"Thanks, sis.

"Oh, I'm sorry, was this supposed to be a giant, happy-family dinner where no one discussed the elephant in the room? Cause, honestly, I feel like it makes things pretty awkward when we all talk like everything is fine.

"Can everyone stop talking for a second? my mom said. "We can talk about these things without immediately attacking each other.

The conversation lulled and we all just waited for someone to break the ice with worthless small talk. I swear to god, the trick to any happy, family relationship is just simply bottling everything up. Just talk about your cousins or the local sports teams or some shit, but the very second it gets on to life aspirations, everyone is fucked. I mean, at least for most people; I'm sure there are a couple people out there who are just absolutely killing it.

Dinner was almost over, I was tired, Reagan was staring at me expectantly. I hit fuck it. "I ODed again.

It was strange. The moments leading up to admitting that had slowed down, as if, somewhere, a pretentious director was slowing down the film so that the audience could truly absorb every moment of tension as I slowly counted down, over and over again, confident that this time would be different. Yet after the words escaped my lips, everything sprung back to real life. No more tension or fear, just a heavy guilt that I marinated in, soaking into every corner of my body.

"When? my dad was the first to speak.

"Last week. Reagan picked me up from the hospital.

My mom got up and left. Reagan looked like she was going to follow, but she reluctantly stayed in her chair. My dad was looking everywhere but me.

My dad just said, "We'll talk about this later, before following my mother out of the room.

"Well, thanks for making my life easier, Reagan said before getting up and leaving. I sat and waited for someone to come back into the room, just for the benefit of conversation, even being berated, just something. After a couple minutes I took one of my dad's beers and went up to my room and tried to sleep.

Chapter 5

I snuck out of my house when I woke up and called one of my roommates after walking out of the neighborhood.

I was sitting on the curb as I felt the sun beat down on the back of my neck. While still recovering from a hangover would be an oversimplification, I nonetheless felt like dogshit. A car honked and I moved back from the street pressing my back to a local church. While the thought of possibly waiting for Naomi in the lobby had piqued my interest, I quickly moved it out of my mind. My thoughts melted together and little seemed pertinent or focused.

Naomi pulled up in an old red SUV and gave the horn a honk startling me. The SUV had been the same one she had since high school and would likely be the only car she would ever drive. She had drunkenly told me that any bumper sticker I bought I could apply to her car. As a result her car was covered in dozens of stickers placed without any thought or theme. I pushed myself to my feet while she beamed at me from inside.

"You dumb asshole, she said as I opened the car door.

She gave me a quick hug and sped off as I closed the door. Her brunette hair had been succinctly put in a ponytail and she was wearing jean cut offs and a 60's band T-shirt, presumably from last night. Her face was surprisingly well framed by purple sunglasses that looked like she had bought them from a pharmacy, although she had most likely stolen them. Her attempt at looking rebellious was completely offset by her smile which always seemed genuine.

"So how's your sister?

"That's your first question?

"Well, what? I haven't seen her in forever and I know you're doing shitty.

"Yeah, I suppose, still.

She gave a smirk as I rummaged around her floor for a phone charger. The floor was littered in fast food bags and assorted trash. I found a bottle of water and carefully smelled it before deciding to drink some. It was warm like bathwater, but I still let it flow down the back of my throat.

"So how is Reagan?

"Pissed.

"Well, duh, but other than being related to a dumbass how's it going?

"I mean pretty well, I think she's finishing up college and should be studying for the MCAT's. Honestly I'm excited for her, she's gonna being doing well.

Naomi shot me a quick smile before cutting off a Buick in traffic. She then pulled an electric cigarette from her dash and the inside of the car permeated with the scent of bubble gum. I tapped her on the shoulder and with a nod she passed the stick. I pulled off my nicotine patch and stuck it to the window. It slowly peeled off and fell to the floor.

"God, I hate this flavor, I said in between smoke clouds.

"Then buy your own, Naomi shot back. "Also Brian did the rest of the coke, but he told me to tell you the paramedics took it.

"Sounds about right.

"Yeah, you didn't hear it from me. Honestly though there was only a couple lines left though, so I wouldn't stress it.

I nodded and let myself sink into the seat. Neat houses and flashy business stood out from among them, offering their unadulterated view of society.

"So did you see anything? Naomi asked.

"What?

"When you ODed, did you see lights or anything?

"I was on a fuck ton of drugs, Naomi.

"That's more the reason you should've seen something.

"No, Naomi, I sighed. "I didn't see anything. I just remember you giving me a shot and then I woke up in the hospital.

"Well that sucks, she replied. "But it's probably a good thing.

"Yeah, sure.

She whipped her SUV into a concrete apartment complex that was now considered home. The apartments had a faded mountain cabin style that had always felt strangely homely to me. I swear I almost took pride in the fact that this urban fiasco was where I lived, free from the pressure of the American dream bullshit. I stumbled out of the car and Naomi shot me a worried glance, only to return to her phone after I gave her a reassuring smile.

We walked past the shallow pool, dying grass, and surprisingly friendly neighbors to get to our porch where we jumped the short wall and onto our property. Perks of the bottom floor. The porch had a hammock, burnt cigarettes, and a couple of plants that Naomi had bought only for me to take care of. We slid open the door and pushed apart the shades to see Brian in the middle of the room taking a bong rip.

The room featured a leather craigslist couch that had constantly peeling strips coming off the top. In front of it was a coffee table with some scattered garbage and two bongs on it, both covered in stickers and rave candi, yet surprisingly well-cleaned. Unlike the table, which was stained in liquor and bong water. The room had a mix of led lights and Christmas lights going around the ceiling like some kind of white trash halo. The rest of the furniture was basically patio furniture all facing away from the TV making the coffee table the epicenter of the room. Every now or then one of us would offer up possible solutions, but the room was likely to stay in it's rotted way 'til we moved out.

"Bro, how you doing?! Brian coughed out as he got up from the couch for a hug. Brian was our other roommate, we'd known him since high school. For a drug dealer he kept his hair cut strikingly short and was well shaven, but aside from that he dressed like how your grandmother would describe a drug dealer.

"Been better.

He let out a cheap laugh, "Yeah I bet, man. You need to learn how to pace yourself. If that chick hadn't been there you'd have had a premature exit.

"Wait, who?

"I don't know some girl you were talking to at the club, you guys came back here after picking up and were still up when we all went to bed. She woke us up freaking out.

Naomi had sat down on the couch and was packing herself a bowl. "Plus she was all coked up and talking like a motorboat.

Brian was laughing, "Yeah, and it took like forty minutes for her roommate to pick her up, you really know how to pick 'em.

Naomi was visibly smirking even with her mouth pressed against the piece. She blew the smoke out and let it slowly dissipate into the air. The little smoke left in the piece floated up from the tip of the glass as if smoke from a gun. Brian sat down next to Naomi and started packing another bowl.

"Fuck, guys, I'm sorry.

"No worries, Naomi shot back.

"Yeah, no sweat, you want some flower? Brian motioned toward the couch next to him. "Nah, I'm okay, I'm just gonna grab a beer and get some more rest.

Brian shrugged and Naomi gave me a smile and a nod. I went into the kitchen (which was uncharacteristically clean) and grabbed a light beer from the fridge. I made my way into my room and collapsed onto my bed. The can hissed and the sound comforted me as I slid off my shoes. I took the scrape of paper from my backpack and tossed them on my desk. The papers were a mixture of literature on addiction and my bill which, unless I won the lottery, would go unpaid until the day I died.

My room was the polar opposite of my room in my parents' house. The mirror that served as the door to my closet was covered in smudges, opposed to the mirror on my desk which was covered in a slight sprinkle, like a frozen pond after a light snow. On my walls hung a tapestry that felt pretentious, a framed poster I stole from a bar, and a series of photos I had taped above my desk. My desk, the sole piece of furniture except for my bed and it's matching chair, was practically unused except as storage for various knickknacks I had acquired.

The far window overlooked the San Francisco Peaks of Flagstaff; the ski trails were still visible in the summer. I remember I looked out at them for at least an hour on some potent shrooms one morning. I took small sips from my beer while scrolling through a little bit of social media before falling asleep on top of the covers.

Chapter 6

Eventually the days became more bearable, the headaches slid away and the feelings of despair became more dialed back to the normal amount of despair that I was used to. I had a few phone calls to make, but mostly it was kept quiet. Naomi believed it was bad karma to gossip and Brian had given me the drugs. Whoever I was with had yet to reach out to me, which was disheartening yet also a relief.

I had asked my boss for a week off and instead he fired me, which was surprisingly comforting. It felt as if it was somehow tainted with my sins of my old mistakes and now I was free to do something new with my life. This reminded me of my oblique optimism I held last time, it would probably fade like last time, although I convinced myself I would hold onto it stronger this time.

I told both Brian and Naomi that I had been fired, neither of whom seemed shocked. It wasn't my first no-call no-show. They offered to help me on rent for a while. I even had to turn down Brian on an offer to help him sell yay for a bit. I know he had only offered out of courtesy, but the idea of stumbling all around the city and dealing with drunks and junkies seemed less than appealing to me.

I would half-heartedly begin the job search online which was always tough as a *shorter*.

Even though it was illegal in this state to "reject applicants for their numbers it only made it illegal for them to be honest with us. The only good news was I had enough experience to seem like I wasn't a complete junkie or anything, even if I wasn't anything special.

That's the worst part about being a *shorter*, the whole chicken or the egg theory. Some believed that anyone who was destined to die before thirty had been chosen by God to die young because he knew they were going to live a life of drugs and sex and general debauchery. Others argued that anyone who found out at eighteen that they had a decade or less to live might not respond in the healthiest of ways and that's where the correlation came from. Personally, I believe that I'm not "cursed by God, but he hasn't ever done me much fucking good.

So for the next week, I got stoned and filled out literally hundreds of job applications online. In between those forms I watched TV and occasionally helped Brian pack drugs.

Brian kept all of his drugs in his room so that if the cops came Naomi and I could plead naivety and avoid prison. It seemed flimsy, but the perks of living with a dealer were currently outweighing the possible negatives. He sold weed, coke, Molly, acid, perks, Adderall (but only to get high, not to study, he had "principles), bars, special-K, and anything else you wanted. If you mentioned any drug he hadn't heard of he would try to order it from one of his various plugs, try it, and then sell it to whoever else wanted it. Mostly he just sold pot and coke to mortals and wasteful college kids though.

We were sitting in his room and I had agreed to help weigh his coke. His desk, which was more a table, had been moved off of the wall and we were sitting on either side. The middle was filled with a scale I had stolen from an old restaurant gig (who I don't use as a reference), a larger pile of blow, and plenty of little baggies. Naomi, who had recently gotten back from her job, was now in sweatpants and laying on his bed.

Her wax pen was floating between the three of us as we talked, mostly for good company.

"How much do you want for this man?

I looked up a Brian quizzically; behind him Naomi mouthed "oh my God as she looked up from her phone.

"Nothing, I'm just helping you out, plus you're helping me with rent. I just needed a break from applying to shit anyways.

"So, you can get paid minimum wage to microwave somebody's food and be miserable again?

"Plus tips, I replied.

"So 'plus tips' just to be miserable?

"Look, I promise you I was plenty miserable before I had a job, okay?

"Actually I remember you being pretty happy, Naomi jumped in. "Like in high school you always seemed pretty carefree. Her face had more of a serious look on it, mixed with something else I couldn't place.

Brian pointed back at her with his thumb as I pushed back against the table. "Just sayin.'

"Not helpful, Naomi.

"Look, I'm not saying sell drugs with dipshit, but maybe figure something out, I feel like you've been a bummer lately.

"First off drugs fix shitty moods so ta-da, Brian said. "Secondly, what do you want him to do, Naomi? You hate your job and get paid shit too.

"Not always. Sometimes I get to play with dogs.

"Look, I jumped in. "If I've been acting like a bummer let's call it a side effect of dying at twenty-seven, okay? Not thrilled with my own morality being shoved in my face.

Naomi laughed and slid her legs off the bed and onto the floor. "I'm dying at 25, bud, you don't get to play that card on me.

"What? Brian exclaimed in faux surprise. "Can I talk at your funeral?

"Will you be on drugs?

"Probably.

"Sure.

Naomi gave Brian a quick high five and they looked at me again. I put my hands up lightly in defeat and dropped into a beanbag chair.

"Look, I'm just not trying to sell drugs. I don't know what I'm doing with my life, but selling drugs ain't part of it, alright?

The two relied with a "whatever, and a "good.

We went back to packing with only Brian's shitty music playing in the background. I don't know whether he had recently been doing too many drugs or whatnot, but his music was slowly becoming a tad bit too eccentric for me even when I was feeling particularly "creative.

"I'm thinking of trying to go sober again.

Naomi looked up and smiled.

Brian just let out a dry laugh. "What's it been, two years? Brian asked.

"Three.

"So you're just gonna get clean?

"I mean slowly, but yeah.

"Okay, well then give me back Naomi's weed pen.

I took another hit while flipping him off.

"No, I think that's good, Naomi chimed in. "Don't be a dick.

"But yeah, what's he getting sober for? To go hiking or some shit?

"Look, what's it matter to you? I just woke up in E.R. for the second time. Shit's getting real.

"So no more beer and weed? Brian asked.

"I'm getting my shit together, not becoming boring.

"Oh, that'll work.

"Hey, man, can't you just say like 'good luck' or something?

"Both of you calm down. Brian don't be a dick, but Danny, Brian has a point.

I looked over at Naomi, she was uncharacteristically serious, again.

"Look, ABCs aside, people do dumb shit when they're drunk; you sure this time it's different?

"ABC's? Brian asked.

"Alcohol becomes cocaine, I replied. "Last time I went fully clean I lasted a couple months. Everyone needs a vice, I just need less.

Naomi looked hesitant. Brian continued packaging.

"I just ... I need a break, okay?

"Okay, I'll hold you to that, Naomi said.

"Whatever, man, Brian replied.

"You know what, package this shit yourself, I said as I stormed out of the room.

* * *

Three weeks later and I was proudly telling everyone I was eight days sober, it fucking sucked. Once the initial frustration and irritation wore off from the detox, it ended up just simply being boring. Sure I was more clearheaded and I spent some time at the gym trying to get healthy, but a runner's high had absolutely nothing on alcohol and cocaine (especially LSD). Unfortunately I had told everyone that I was gonna go a month, so now I was stuck in the middle of it.

So here I was on the patio reading cause I had nothing

better to do. Just sipping on coffee and already on my second cigarette. My addiction had segued into more acceptable drugs. Coffee and cigarettes, the church man's cocaine. That being said unless you were gonna die after forty years, no one gave a shit if you smoked. Might as well go to town on your lungs at that point.

Naomi came out of her room and I waved at her before yelling, "Yo, can you grab me one of those IPA's I bought the other day?!

She gave me a thumbs-up and grabbed one from the fridge She came out and tossed it to me while sitting in one of the cheap lawn chairs across from me.

"Those taste alright?

"For non-alcoholic they actually taste pretty good, just helps with the cravings. How you doing this morning?

She shrugged and pulled out a joint. She snagged the lighter from our table, before awkwardly looking at me. I waved for her to proceed and she lit up. Smoking openly was probably grounds for a fine, especially since we were on the first floor, but we had yet to get a fine so we just went for it, even if what we were smoking was less than legal.

"Whatcha reading?

"Just an old sci-fi novel I've been meaning to get around to, figured might as well now.

"I thought you were supposed to read the newspaper with coffee.

"Well, the news is all about the Let-Them-Serve-Bill and we're fucked.

"I mean I don't read the news except for Twitter, but if we were gonna go to war with Europe or something anytime soon I'd have heard about it. We're probably fine.

"Probably, I agreed.

Essentially shorters were drafted at a higher rate ever since society found out a way to look at people's numbers about a hundred years ago. The argument was that they were gonna die early anyways so might as well shove us all on the front lines. Another argument was made that this would lower crime rates back in the home country while the war raged, which in my mind was toying with the idea of eugenics. Unsurprisingly a bunch of like-minded individuals and special interest groups found some issue with this law and were consistently trying to get it repealed. Unfortunately they were getting their asses kicked.

"Well how's sobriety going? Naomi asked breaking my thoughts.

"Boring, I said honestly.

"Well, wanna do something? I'm free all day.

"Actually, can you do me a favor?

She shrugged. "Sure.

* * *

"So what's the number?

I flipped my phone around and showed Naomi my screen and she began dialing the number. She clicked the speaker button and plopped her phone down on the table. She had just woken up and was wearing a T-shirt of Brian's that had shrunken in the dryer and gym shorts. She took a big gulp of our apartment complex's free coffee, although it was doubtful that it actually did much.

"Try to sound professional, okay?

"I know how to talk you di— Hey, is Thomas there?

"That's me, who is this?

"Hi, my name is Audrey and I work for Burger King and we're hiring for a dishwasher, Naomi replied.

I immediately threw my hands up in protest as Naomi flipped me off and made a faux smile.

"Can I ask you about Daniel Brooker? He recently applied to work here and he used you as a reference.

"He used me for a reference?

"Mm-hmm.

"I mean he's a decent worker, doesn't make problems with staff or employees, but he's definitely a stereotypical shorter.

"What do you mean?

"Oh, you know, probably a junkie, usually hungover or taking suspicious bathroom breaks, stuff like that.

"Oh, really?

"Yeah, good luck with that.

Thomas succinctly hung up and I laid back down on my couch with a thump.

"Fuck, I thought he actually liked me.

"Well, he did seem to like you ...

"If he actually liked me he would be willing to lie to a Burger King for me, which by the way I appreciate that improvisation.

"It seemed like a realistic opportunity for you.

"Thanks.

Naomi shrugged as I scratched him off the list of possible references. "So 'suspicious bathroom breaks?'

"I promise you I don't do drugs at work, I'm just on my phone and stuff during downtime.

"Okay ... I don't care.

"So, I guess I'm using you as a recommendation again.

"Duh, Naomi rolled her eyes and reached for the bong on

the table. She let some flower fall into the bowl as she packed her morning hit.

"Just remember that you're a manager at Beaver Street and that I was a phenomenal waiter.

"Right, and I'll just tell 'em that the only reason you don't work for us anymore is that you couldn't handle the biweekly fight clubs.

"Right, but only because I wouldn't stoop to the level of steroids, I replied as I preceded to alter my resume on my laptop.

"Sure, Naomi said as she finished packing her bong. "Honestly, I don't understand why you don't have me and Brian just lie in the first place, like why bother finding out if these fuckheads actually would give you the time of day?

"Well, firstly, honesty is a virtue and I don't know, I'd like to think that they liked me even if they fired me for throwing up at work or sleeping through a shift.

"Oh my god that is some classic Taurus shit.

"You know, I have no idea what that means.

"Oh right, cause you don't believe in anything, her eyes rolled as she spoke.

"I just haven't done as many shrooms as you have.

"Your loss, Naomi said as she pressed the edge of the bong to her lips and began to flick the lighter. The sparks jumped as a single lonely flame burnt the edges of the bowl causing the bright green to turn black and shrivel. With a cough the smoke was transferred from the piece into the living room as the coughing turned into giddy laughter.

"I know, I'd just like to imagine that even someone who thought I was a shitty employee would still be rooting for me ya know. Like why not just lie for me?

Naomi shrugged and went back to the kitchen to pull a water from the fridge. "Do you need to borrow money?

"No, thanks for offering though.

Naomi stifled a laugh. "I don't have money, I was going to tell you to ask Brian.

"I think I owe him money.

"Well, if you need more, he's got it.

* * *

One of the perks of living with a drug dealer was the fact that he had an abundance of money and drugs. As an addict I was in constant need of both. While waiting tables should give any twenty year old kid as much money as he or she should need, I rarely found myself in the black.

Brian grew up an adrenaline junkie. Whether that was pouring lighter fluid on fireworks or trying to ride a shopping cart down the biggest hill in the neighborhood, he was doing one thing after another. So as he grew up he gained a few broken bones and a reputation for generally being a dumbass. This carried into high school, where I first met him, when we were grouped together for a history class. I did my half mostly last minute and sent it to Brian, I found out later he did his half at lunch and we scraped by with a C.

I was a little pissed, but didn't care enough to make a deal out of it. The few parties I went to before I got my digits I usually saw him there, his reputation for stealing booze from grocery stores worked as an invite in of itself. Eventually I knew him as a nice enough kid although his future priorities were strictly limited to enjoying himself and getting plastered. No judgement from my end, plenty of high school kids are like that.

After my digits, Naomi reintroduced me to him as her pot dealer. The first time I picked up he asked me to roll up my sleeve. Pretty sure afterwards he was telling everyone about how "the straight edge kid was showing his true colors. I tended to avoid him except when I was picking up and if it wasn't for me being friends with Naomi I'm sure he would've avoided me too.

Toward the end of the year he got his numbers and found out he was gonna die at 34. He sought Naomi and I out; ended up having a midlife crisis just like both of us had months prior.

We told him a bunch of bullshit about how it wasn't that bad and things of that nature. Within a couple of months we were all buying fake IDs together and a few years later we were living together. The longest he ever hld a job was three months at a Dairy Queen.

Eventually he gave up trying to have a straight job.

* * *

I held in the smoke as I softly pulled my puff from my lips. I slowly sucked it down my throat and then let it seep out of my nose before leaning back into the seat. Naomi was sitting in the shotgun seat talking the ear off the uber driver as I slid my Puff over to Brian. He gratuitously nodded and did the same. Although I'm sure the scent of synthetic apples was permeating the car, the driver said nothing about it when he dropped us off downtown. Brian tossed the stick to Naomi and we started walking toward the bar.

The first place we were coming to was called the Monte Vista Lounge. Basically a pretty standard dive bar except someone hired a DJ a couple years ago and suddenly it's a massive draw for shitty people like us.

The air was crisp on my skin as we walked through the little hub that housed 2:00 a.m. bars. My jacket had been abandoned at our apartment to show off my T-shirt and in the hopes that the clubs would be crowded enough to keep me warm. Brian was similarly dressed and was absentmindedly rubbing his arms as Naomi was staring into storefronts we passed by.

"Look, I don't see why we can't just uber straight to the bar every time it's your turn to call it, I said to Brian.

"Dude, if Uber thinks that we're going to just some random bookstore they won't jack up the price as compared to if you're going to a bar. They track that shit, man.

"Yeah they don't, but I like the occasional walk, Naomi chirped in.

"Just pay the three bucks next time. I've seen what you charge kids, you can afford it.

"You can pay it, Brian replied. "What are you cold or something?

"I mean, yeah, a little.

"Should've drank beforehand like us, Brian said.

"Uh-huh.

We kept walking and passed an obnoxiously loud street preacher shouting and holding up a sign that succinctly informed us that we were all going to hell. Brian gave him a quick thumbs-up in overly exaggerated manner much to Naomi's delight.

"God is gonna send you to hell for mocking him! You need to repent for your sins!

"Hey, check this out, Naomi yelled as she pulled up her right sleeve and revealed her numbers which read February

20th, almost three years from now. She also showed half a tattoo of a vintage-style fem devil which probably wasn't the main focus of the man's anger, but surely didn't improve his temperament. His eyes sharpened and he took a step forward to seemingly try to smack away the numbers. Naomi quickly pulled her arm away and jumped back while stifling a giggle. Simultaneously, I grabbed Brian who was lunging at the man.

"Chill, man, I'm not trying to get arrested this early.

"You're a mortal because God is angered with your sins!

"I'm gonna kick your ass if you try that again! Brian yelled at him while I slowly started pushing him in the opposite direction.

The man continued yelling and pointing at us as Naomi waved at him while walking backward. His voice faded away to the background as we turned the corner and kept walking.

"Bro, I wish he would've done something again and I would've swung on him.

"It's not worth it man, guy's just a nut job. Just get a good laugh at him and be thankful you're not as dumb as he is, I said.

Brian continued venting while Naomi and I went to our phones and followed along half-heartedly. Those guys always made me laugh, yet I've always felt strangely sympathetic toward them. Just a sad lonely man angry at the world, needing someone to blame. Just so desperate for human interaction that he's trying to start shit just to feel a connection with someone.

On the other hand he's an asshole, so usually my feelings fade once they open their mouths or I get close enough to read their preachy signs. God hates fags, shorters, and anyone else who doesn't have my exact limited world view. Smoking the marijuana will make you gay. Fun stuff like that and I can't help but laugh. I always like the idea of them going into a craft store filled with soccer moms and hippies, just muttering away about God's vengeance as they sort through a bin of markers trying to figure out which shade of blue will really make their signs pop.

We came to the downtown Monte Vista Lounge and settled into the line waiting toward the entrance. The people in line were mostly college kids and assholes dressed like us, always one weird forty-year-old guy trying to fit in, awkwardly chatting people up. When we finally reached the front we showed the bouncer our IDs before quickly dropping down into the bar. The stairwell's walls were brick and featured various older photographs from over the years. They all portrayed the same attitude of a bar that would make you reminiscent of the Cheer's theme song. Once you reached the bottom and turned the corner however, the Lounge's former identity was turned into merely a ghost as lights blasted through the entrance, splattering the walls behind me in neon blurbs. We began pushing through the crowd trying to make our way to the bar.

I could feel the music pulsing if I placed my hand against my chest. My eyes were adjusting to the dark and flashes as I managed to push one hand onto the bar top and hold a spot. Naomi and Brian shouted their orders at me as I waited for one of the bartenders to catch my eye. I made a few half assed attempts to make conversation with the girl next to me before resigning to my position. When my drinks arrived I slugged back my shot before bringing the rest back over to Naomi and Brian.

I handed a Red Bull vodka to Brian and a cranberry vodka to Naomi. The green bottle in my hand glinted at Brian.

"You drinking tonight?

I held up the bottle of O'Doul's and shook my head. Brian

blew a raspberry before turning around to push through the crowd. Naomi and I followed as we began our march through the congested masses. We turned the corner of the bar to see a DJ standing above the crowd, behind him a large screen projected laughing skulls with a hypnotism swirl circling behind them.

Brian apparently knew someone who had bought some table upfront and we began pushing our way toward them. Sure enough as we shoved our way there to the side of the dance floor was a semi-packed table with a few recognizable faces. Most notably was Billy, who was as white trash as it gets short of fucking your cousin. He was drinking from a top shelf bottle of tequila that was either brazenly snuck in or foolishly bought.

Billy saw Brian and motioned us up and we climbed into the elevated booth, giving Brian a hug, me a fist bump, and a fist bump and smirk to Naomi who had decided to ignore it. I took a quick pull from the tequila as the bottle was passed around. Brian and Billy broke off to talk shop while Naomi and I melted into the group at the table.

Brian referred to Billy as a coworker, not a friend. Nonetheless we saw him too often. He was either trying to hit on Naomi or convince me to sell drugs for him. In both regards he expected us to be in awe of his genius and refused to understand we weren't interested.

"Since when can Billy afford this shit I yelled to Naomi over a soulless remix of Tupac. "Oh, who knows, he's probably trying to fuck a girl out of his league. Let's just stay up here and enjoy it for a minute.

I nodded and continued sipping on my fake beer as I let my foot tap along to the beat. Naomi was talking about a mutual friend who had recently done something or another and I nodded along half-heartedly. Virtually everyone we knew at this point was a fuck up on one level or another. I remembered my own slow descent into fuckuppery after I had gotten my numbers. While there were a few mild exceptions to those of who slipped to the outskirts of society, most of us were shorters. That's more or less how I met Naomi.

The bottle rounded back to me and I took a second to inspect the label before passing it along to Naomi who took a swig and tried to secretly nurse it for a second. Another girl noticed and Naomi reluctantly handed it over after taking a last sip. I glanced over the dance floor looking for familiar faces or a girl I might have a shot with.

Naomi was gripping my arm tightly as she swiveled me in front of a girl I think named Kelly. The girl was wearing an overpriced hoodie and booty shorts. Naomi had started talking to her before pulling me into the conversation. Kelly looked both ways, more for show than anything else, before leaning in with a smirk.

"Look, I'm not friends with Billy. Whenever he sells me drugs he's always trying get me to come out and usually I say no but he said he had a table and I figured why not bring a couple of friends. He'll probably try to hit on me, but, whatever, right?

"Okay, sure, I replied.

Kelly seemed to notice Naomi's furrowed eyebrows and with an eye roll she carried on. "Anyways your friend was wondering since when dipshit had the money to buy a table, my friend Justin who used to sell with him says that supposedly he made a *pact* with some suppliers down in Phoenix.

Kelly stepped back and her smirk grew wider. "How crazy is that, right?

I looked over to Naomi who was serious. She stared at Billy who was dancing drunkenly about ten feet away. We made eye contact and she briefly shook her head before looking back over at him.

"We're not responsible for any of it, plus it's not like we can do anything.

"What? I was now looking back at Kelly who had replaced her smirk with crossed arms and a glare.

"We can't do anything, there's not even a way to prove anything so you don't have to act like I'm an asshole.

"Okay, yeah, sorry, whatever.

I turned away from her and me and Naomi started walking back toward the bar. I sensed Kelly was shooting me daggers from behind, but I purposefully ignored it. We stood behind the masses at the bar, but didn't really make an effort to move forward, which felt like it rang true in a deeper sense.

"So, do you think it's true?

"No, Brian wouldn't stay around someone like that.

"Well, yeah, but he might not know. Hold up, let me try something.

I pushed my way to the bar again and got ahold of the bartender again.

"Hey can you get our table another bottle? I asked.

"Make it a surprise, just make sure it's something nice.

I pointed to the table and the bartender reluctantly sent his barback over. "Hey, Naomi, stand away from me for a second.

I stood alone at the bar as the barback got up next to Billy and yelled in his ear, before pointing at me. I gave an enthusiastic wave, to which Billy shrugged and gave me a huge thumbs-up. I gave him a thumbs-up back before returning telling the bartender to add a generous tip on Billy before returning to Naomi.

"What'd you tell them to get?

"Something expensive that'd he'd never pay on someone like me.

"Drunk people make dumb decisions ...

"Not for guys like me. I turned to face Naomi. "I'm gonna talk to Brian.

I pushed my way back over to him. He was sitting in the booth, slowly dancing to the beat. I sat down next to him and he quickly turned, excited to see me.

"Yo man there's a rumor that Billy just signed a *pact,* did you hear any shit like?!

Brian scratched the back of his head and nodded at a girl as she walked off. "Yeah, bro, but c'mon, you don't think he'd ever do shit like that?

"I don't know, I've never known him to be a paragon of moral superiority.

"Look we'll figure it out later, I'm just trying to have a good time, okay?

"Yeah same, just ... look I don't wanna be around people like that.

"Dude, even if he had, we're not even like accomplices or anything.

His brows were now creased and his tone had sharpened. I took a deep breath and began trying to count to ten before replying.

"Fuck you, man. I want no part of this shit.

I turned around and started heading back toward Naomi before being shoved in the back. I bumped into a girl whose red drink splashed onto my shirt. I turned around to see Brian standing defiantly with his feet planted, he looked sad though. I felt eyes on me and hoped none were a bouncer's. I slowly turned back around, ignoring the glare of the girl I bumped into and found Naomi.

"We're leaving; he's staying.

"Are you serious? I barely heard her whisper.

"Yup.

She grabbed a tequila bottle off the table, taking an overexaggerated pull before passing it to me. I slammed some back before placing it on the table sideways, letting the liquor spill out onto the table. Some guy on the other end of the table looked like he was gonna try to hit me, but Brian held him back. We briefly made eye contact before I turned around. I pushed through the crowd as I followed Naomi toward the door. We were only followed by a handful of empty threats and Brian congratulating me on my sobriety. A bouncer was watching us dutifully, but let us pass to the exit.

Chapter 7

"Do you really think he made a Pact?

"I don't fucking know, but without a straightforward answer I'm not sticking around. Besides he's an asshole anyways.

Naomi shrugged and put a cigarette in her mouth we had gotten from a nearby smoke shop. I motioned toward them and she gave me one before sliding them back into her jeans.

"Careful, those will kill you before you hit fifty.

I smirked as I lit the cigarette. We were walking farther downtown toward another club that hopefully housed a more agreeable type of degenerates.

A pact was simple enough, not a creative name, but the thugs that did them probably weren't the most creative types. Essentially you got paid X amount of money, then a couple years down the line when you were a week or so before your numbers were gonna act up, you did what they wanted you to do. Rob a bank, smuggle scarface levels of drugs, kill someone, etc. Always something dangerous and unethical that no one would ever do, unless you only got a week or so to live.

Everyone had heard of them, some dipshit always ended up on the news for a felony with a week left on his clock. They almost never talked, hardly any time left on their wrist so they'd just wait to die in order to protect whoever they were protecting. Occasionally, you'd hear about some poor son of a bitch getting shot cause the guy with a pact had run off. So whoever was unlucky enough to be the collateral got to pay the debt their "friend or family member owed.

Rarely, any criminals or cops actually chalk it up to pacts

cause there is no way to prove it, but everyone knows. News stations play it for ratings and sets society spiraling into a moral panic for a week. There's been massive debates about how to stop it. Cops watching suspicious shorters as they wind down, but that just moves the day for action up a week and doesn't usually stop much. Some backward countries even allow torture on criminals suspected of making a pact, something even the most liberal of people like myself have a hard time arguing against.

They never get any real information out of anybody, but I suspect that's not why people are for it. They just want to thrash out at anything cruel in the world even if it can't change anything, but unknowingly, themselves.

I tried to shake off the thoughts of Billy as I flicked the ashes off the tip of my cigarette. Sure enough the liquor had acted as a coat and I hardly noticed the cold as we walked down the street.

"I'm probably not gonna drink at the next bar, so don't feel like you have to, Naomi said.

"That's okay. I was probably gonna drink anyways, I replied.

"Well let me know if you want to stop and go home.

I nodded and thanked her.

We walked into a bar that was a sports bar by day but had moved all of their tables into the corner. It was never known to be the best spot but we were more afraid of losing our momentum more than anything else at this point. The bar was crowded enough, just enough people to keep the atmosphere fun.

I saw a girl in the crowd smoking a small cigarette. She was flicking it slightly while trying to keep it hidden behind her jacket. She had curly blond hair that was cut just under her shoulders and a mischievous smile that was countered by her friends glare. Her friend was continually looking over her shoulder and whispering something at her. The girl with the cigarette took a comically long pull before letting it fall to the ground and have the embers extinguished by a twist of her boot.

"Hey, Naomi, I'm gonna go over and shoot my shot.

"Who?

"Curly hair in the boots.

Naomi smirked.

"Let me know if she's gay.

"For sure. See you tomorrow.

"Yeah more like ten minutes.

Naomi laughed as I flipped her off before heading deeper into the crowd. I took another sip of my beer before I reached her. I pushed through the crowd and tapped her on the shoulder.

She turned around and stared at me blankly.

"Hey, I've got a light, do you mind if I bump a cig?

Her friend immediately cut in, pushing herself in between the two of us. "Uh, no, we're gonna be leaving. Pretend she has a dick or something. C'mon Tierra, let's go.

The girl smiled. "I don't know, I think I could go for a smoke, she said while looking straight back at me. Her friend snorted before letting go of her and pushing back into the crowd.

"Well, your friend seems fun, I said motioning toward the wake that was quickly filling in behind her.

"Oh, she's just pissy cause her boyfriend's not texting her back, she replied while pulling out another cigarette. "Honestly, I think you'd like her.

"So, can I buy you a drink? I asked with a light chuckle.
"Sure, but only if she's watching. Serves her right.
"Works for me.

* * *

We were in her car that was parked on the curb a couple blocks away from the downtown area. The car was hidden somewhat from the street lamps by the large pine trees hugging the curb, but I sensed she didn't much care if we were seen. House remixes of old pop songs were playing through her radio as I leaned back into the leather of the passenger seat. The car was an old Lexus with a faded blue exterior. Presumably her parents', but I hadn't asked.

Her name was Tierra and explained that she was from Nevada despite her fake ID saying Chicago. She was a sophomore at NAU and presumably didn't give a fuck about school, although I had been surprised by people's grades before.

She rolled down her window to ash her cigarette and a crisp breeze floated in and the car began to permeate with the smell of conifers. It was a surprisingly peaceful feeling and a small smile formed on my face. Tierra glanced over and rolled her eyes.

"C'mon, pass the bullet.

I passed over the small silver vial about the size of a pen cap. The paint was dull and the singular button was faded. Tierra placed her finger on the hole, flipped it, and then inhaled it through her nostril. She took a deep breath and smiled before letting out a quick exhale. I slid it back into my pockets while she placed her thumb against her nose just in case she hadn't thoroughly gotten high.

"That's good shit, where'd you get it.

"Oh a kid I know from high school has some connect down in Phoenix or something, I lied. Real answer was from Naomi who I texted while Tierra was in the bathroom. She got it from Brian, who did in fact get it from someone in Phoenix (I think).

"Neat, do you think I could get another hit?

I reached back into my pocket and gave it to her. She shot another hit up her opposite nostril before tossing it back to me. I slid it back into my pocket.

"You're not gonna take another hit?

"Nah, I think I'm good for a while.

She shrugged and began to tinker with her nose again. I pushed away the urge to try and take another hit. I rubbed my palm against my chest and felt my heart beating away, understanding the need to steam ahead as it was directed. I took a deep breath and glanced back at Tierra.

"So what do you do?

"You mean besides this?

"Yeah, besides geeking on my blow, what do you do?

"Psych major, classes aren't too hard so I can just do this every weekend.

"I think it's ironic that only crazy girls take those classes.

"Fuck you, she gave me a playful push. "Anyways, yeah, I'm just gonna coast through college and then who the fuck knows. You?

"Currently in the middle of the who-the-fuck-knows. I feel like everyone is always kinda in that mode though.

"Well, yeah, but what do you do?

"Waiter, but it's actually not that bad.

"Oh I bet.

I flipped her off and she pretended to be aghast. We both leaned back into her chairs, the music filled the silence as I filled my mouth with guava flavored smoke. The nicotine was more for comfort, I had too much in my body for it to do much of anything else. I took a deep breath, then did a mock look around outside.

"Hey, doing shit in the middle of this neighborhood seems a bit sketch. Wanna try to dip?

"Yeah, sure, my roommate is a cunt. Let's go to your place.

She sat up and turned her keys in the ignition. The car lights flipped on, flashing their lights across the streets, breaking the illusion of our privacy. I went to reach for the wheel and suggest an uber, but I settled down into my seat again. She jerked out of her parking spot and began coasting down the street.

Tierra turned the radio way up, blasting the electronic music way the fuck up. I could feel the door shake on the side of my leg.

I saw the inner of her right forearm was illuminated by the dashboard as her jacket ever so slightly slid down her wrist. It was pale and plain, like a page in a newly bought sketch book. I swore to myself lightly and I could feel Tierra look at me suspiciously.

"What? she asked while slightly turning down the radio.

"Your wrist, it's empty, I replied.

"Yeah, something wrong with that? she said, taking her eyes off the road to smirk at me.

"Pull over.

"What?

"Pull over *now*.

"Why?

"Cause I'm not trying to get arrested for giving coke to a 17 year old.

"Oh my God. Chill. I'm just left handed.

She flashed her numbers briefly at me on her left hand while laughing as I sagged back into my seat. I couldn't help but briefly see some of her numbers before I started to briefly chuckle in relief.

"Sorry I just didn't see any numbers or gnostic symbols ..

"No, you're fine. I like messing with guys about that. A couple guys didn't freak out which was a big red flag, but, yup I'm twenty so, no worries.

I laughed again, "Glad to hear it, I said. "By the way did I see a ninety?

Her smirk faded a little, I knew I should apologize and change the subject, but I was too drunk or high or both to not pry.

"Maybe, but why do you care?

"Just curious I suppose, I said.

"Well why?

"I don't know. I just am I guess.

"Well, learn to live with disappointment.

I put my hands up defensively and began staring out the window. The trees were flipping by as I listened to the music. I was expecting her to break the awkward silence, but she seemed comfortable in it, letting it soak into the atmosphere.

"You know if your number really is ninety you should probably do less coke.

"Do you wanna get thrown out of the car?

"Look, I'm just saying I've known people who've gone too hard and then suddenly they're found face down in their room with blood dripping down their face.

"Well, they sound like pussies who can't handle their drugs.

"Fuck you. I've overdosed and I'm lucky to be here, okay? See my numbers?

I held out my arm and pulled up my sleeve revealing my numbers. In small black numbers perpendicular to my wrist the numbers **5 5 27** were branded into me.

The numbers themselves were plain yet haunting in their simplicity. After I got them I began wearing long-sleeved shirts more often or a cluster of tacky bracelets to hide them. I told others (and myself) that it was to hide it from strangers and protect myself from the perceptions that they would push onto me. Not that hiding them removed them from my mind.

"See that? I'm gonna die May 5th and I'm gonna be twenty-seven. If I clock out early in some dive bar with blood running out my nose nobody is gonna give a shit. If you throw sixty years of life out for some dumb high it's a waste.

She pulled over and stopped the car. I had to throw my hand onto the dash to keep my forehead from bouncing off the windshield.

"Look, if you think you're not wasting your life, too, you're a fucking idiot. I do drugs cause life is boring and I wanna get fucked up, not because I'm some self-pitying narcissist who thinks he's rebelling when all he is a walking cliché.

"I'm just saying ...

"I don't care. Get out of my car.

"Look I'm trying to help you.

"Yeah, I'm sure you always embrace help with open arms. Get the fuck out of my car.

I took a deep breath and opened the car door, a breeze of cool air swept across my face. I turned around and Tierra was staring at me, she motioned toward the door. I took a step back and shut the door in a grand dramatic gesture. She slammed on the gas speeding forward, braked slightly causing the door to snap forward then slam shut before driving off.

I waited before eventually being thoroughly convinced that she was gone to pull out my phone to call Naomi.

"Yo, what's up?!

"Hey, I'm guessing you aren't sober so I can't get a ride .." I replied.

I heard her laugh on the other end.

"Wanna come get fucked up at this chick's house with her roommate? She has a turtle.

I checked the time on my phone while I could hear an unidentified person yelling for me not be a pussy before putting it back to my ear.

"Sure, what's the addy?

Chapter 8

I was woken up by a nosebleed. I instinctively rubbed the blood off and it smeared across the polyester couch I was on. The couch was a light brown and the blood left a dark patch. I glanced around, seeing a couple of other stains, I rolled over and tried to shut my eyes again. I couldn't quite remember exactly anything so I figured if it was important it'd come to me in the morning. It was morning, I just meant my morning.

I was woken up whenever later by Naomi shoving my shoulder harshly. I turned over to see her hair looking matted. She had an ever so slight grin on her face and she kept pushing me even though I was clearly up.

"Yo, sleepyhead, time to skedaddle.

"Oh, for fuck's sake, what time is it?

"Two, and I already called the Uber so let's go.

I sat up and glanced around the room. The room had a slick feel to it, or would if it wasn't so dirty.

The table in front of me had a few still full beer cans and an empty handle. Everyone else had either vacated or gone back to their room.

"Fuck, what happened?

"Oh you know the same old. C'mon let's go.

"I gotta wipe that stain off first.

"Shit, get your crap, I'll do it real fast.

* * *

We got to our apartment block and the uber driver dropped us off. I popped in the gate code as Naomi kept walking. I nearly slipped on ice as we were walking through the parking lot.

"I swear to God, I'm gonna vomit. Naomi laughed while hitting her e-cig.

"I swear to God you are the biggest bitch I know. Just wait till we get back to our apartment so our neighbors don't know what a pussy you are.

"Fuck off, I'll puke in your room.

"Yeah, whatever. Naomi took another hit, "So things really go that badly with that one chick?

"What, they went fine, we just exchanged numbers is all.

"You came over and said she was crazy and that you'd totally have hit that if you didn't care about her.

Naomi looked over at me with her eyebrows raised.

"Alright, I saw her numbers. They had her at ninety. I said maybe, just maybe she should do less coke.

Naomi started laughing again. "You dumb piece of shit, why do you care what she does?

"It's just the principle, like she's got her whole life ahead of her and she's just wasting it on drugs. We were fucked by the cosmos, I said pointing at the two of us.

"You sound like your parents.

"Fuck off, we're different.

"Okay.

We hopped over our little patio wall and slid open the door back into our apartment. "You know for someone who deal's drugs you'd think Brian would want us to lock that door more.

Naomi shrugged and plopped down on the couch as I headed to the kitchen. A collection of dirty plates laid in the sink which I ignored. I pulled some pop tarts out and dropped them in our toaster.

"You need breakfast?

"Nah, I'm good, Naomi replied from the couch. "Wait don't you have work today?

"No I start tomorrow, thank God. I'm not pulling this shit the night before my first shift. Naomi laughed as I sat down on the couch next to her.

"So it really doesn't bother you when people with an actual shot at life live like us?

"Oh my God, you're such a fucking pessimist you know that?

"Look what can we do with our lives? I can't go to college cause I can't get a loan. I can't raise kids... It makes sense for us. But people like that are wasting their lives.

"Everyone knows they're gonna die. You think everyone else isn't constantly aware of their own morality? You're just mad cause you'd like to think you'd be different so it's ruining your excuse to be lazy and to relapse.

"Okay, point made, but look at you. Naomi leaned back into the couch and looked at me with the "you trying to get hit expression. "You were in honors in high school, you had gotten drunk like maybe once tops, you were a devout Waterson, you think that was all coming to a crashing halt if you found out you were gonna live to ninety.

"Hey, my parents are devout Watersons, I was just along for the ride, you know how kids are.

"Okay, that seems convenient.

"Oh, fuck you. You didn't actually know me in high school until we were seniors, you just knew the fucking image of me. So don't pretend like you would've understood exactly who I was or where I was going. You're just the kid who could hardly go a week sober.

"But, am I wrong?

"Yeah. And sometimes it's better to keep your mouth shut. You're not my fucking therapist. She got up and headed toward her room. "Your Pop-Tarts are burning.

"Ah, fuck me. I got up and ran toward the kitchen as I heard Naomi slam her door behind herself.

* * *

She was right though, I didn't really know her in high school until the last year. She was quiet, but definitely smart, honors classes and all. I knew her parents were devout Watersons and she hung around with kids who mostly came from that same background. Met her a couple times, but never actually had a conversation with her. Seemed nice enough, just hung out with different people is all.

She was the first person, our year, to actually be a shorter.

Every senior class is filled with tons of kids anxious to get their dates and even more anxious to see what everyone else got. A couple kids got their numbers over the summer, but there was no huge surprises. A kid named Greg got his late August and found out he was gonna die at 54, but that was nothing too scary. More sad than anything else. Last I heard he graduated college a year early and was more or less doing okay.

Naomi was mid-September. She turned eighteen and called in sick for almost a week, so everyone figured something was up. No Instagram post announcing her date or anything either. People started talking immediately, by the third day rumors

were everywhere. Her closest friends refused to talk to anyone and some of the more devout kids kept claiming that she
was too kind for a bad date, that it was just a coincidence.
When she finally came back on Tuesday a week later she was
wearing a sweatshirt with the right sleeve cut off below the
elbow so everyone could see her date, more balls than I had.
She left during her second period and wasn't seen for another
two days.

Most of her friends were more than supportive, to the
point of a couple of fights breaking out for even the simplest
of jokes. Some of her "friends claimed that God had seen
something that they hadn't and immediately stopped associat-
ing themselves with her. A few followed them a couple weeks
after.

Just like that she became the most talked about person in
the school. She sat in the same spot with her remaining friends
that she always had and people couldn't help but flock to her.
Just coming up and asking for advice about getting their own
numbers or trying to be kind and tell her that everything was
going to be okay. One kid named Jack (complete fucking asshole) convinced himself that she was secretly a sex addict and
that's why she was being punished. He got his balls kicked
clean into his stomach when he tried to get her to sleep with
him in the parking lot. I'm sure she hated the attention, but
there was nothing she could do about it.

I was the third kid in my class to find out that I was fucked.
Late November birthday, a kid named Nathaniel found out he
was gonna die at 31 in between us. She found me as soon as
she heard and gave me her number, the both of us ignoring
the whispers going on around us. She made a groupchat with
Nathaniel and I and took me out for coffee later to try to pre-

pare me for everything. We kept adding unlucky souls to the groupchat as the year went on. Got up to eight kids, including Brian who didn't find out 'til March. Chat is still going, nothing much more than dumb jokes and internet memes at this point though.

We started occasionally hanging out after that, but by the time May rolled around we were practically seeing each other everyday. My best friend Luke was there all the time too, pretty sure the two of them were secretly hooking up. As he went off to college across the country, though, we drifted apart, which was a shame but pretty predictable in retrospect. So then slowly but surely most of my friends became shorters like me.

* * *

I heard Brian come home as I was watching TV on my bed. He shortly knocked on my door.

"Hey, you home, man?

"Yeah. Give me a second. I slid my laptop over and shut it, the voice of an overenthusiastic comedian deafened as I put my feet on the floor and walked over. I opened the door to a surprisingly put together Brian, still wearing the clothes from last night along with his backpack, but looking rather refreshed.

"Where were you, man?

"Oh, I left pretty quickly after you guys left and went over to Kat's. Naomi home?

I nodded and he went over to her room, dropping his backpack off on the kitchen counter.

I sank into the living room couch as he did the same to Naomi's door. I played with my phone daring it to try to keep me moderately entertained for the time being. Naomi came out and I shrugged when she looked at me. She sat down on the couch next to me as Brian got ready for whatever he felt he needed to say.

"Look, I was drunk and I was acting like an asshole. I've known Billy for a long time and he didn't seem like the type of person to sign a pact, okay?

"Did he? I asked.

"Just let me finish. It's just I think I'm a good person and just because I'm a drug dealer doesn't mean I'm bad. I just hate how everyone assumes I'm an asshole just because I sell drugs.

"You are an asshole, Naomi said and I snickered.

"Look I'm trying to be real with you guys for a second, can you please chill? We quieted down and I put my hands up in faux surrender.

"Just I get defensive when anyone just assumes that all drug dealers are sociopaths cause I feel like we're not. Anyways that's why I got pissed last night, but you were right. He got drunk and told me he made a pact for money. He's a piece of shit.

The air got sucked out of the room. We all sat silently for someone to break the moment. Brian was fidgeting with one of his bracelets as he stood waiting for whatever we were gonna say. Obviously we'd heard about pacts in rumors and in Waterson propaganda and such, but this type of straight admission felt different.

"Well, I'm going to the cops, Naomi blurted out.

"You can't, Brian replied.

"Why not?

"No proof; it's our word against his. It would just put on his fucking radar, I said, unfortunately agreeing with Brian.

"They already sent him the money probably or something, right?

"Not to his bank account or anything, said Brian.

"How about you shut the fuck up, okay? Naomi shot back at Brian. She was standing up now and holding her bong in her hand making her knuckles white. It hung like a mace, the stale water sloshing in the bottom as a crashing wave.

"Naomi, I said, also getting up in case I needed to put myself between her and Brian. "We can call the cops on him for dealing drugs. That should work.

"He's gonna kill someone, Danny.

"I know, I said

"He might just do something like— Brian tried saying before being cut off by Naomi.

"He's just fucking waiting 'til he's got a week left and then he's gonna kill someone.

"Look, Brian, when he told you this shit, do you think anyone else knew?

"He said it to a couple girls along with me and some guy I didn't know. I think he was bragging.

"See there we go, I said to Naomi. "He's a complete fucking moron and he won't be able out to figure out who ratted on him. We tell the cops, they'll lock him up for drugs, then he'll spend the rest of his days in a jail cell. Does that work for you?

"He'll probably end up killing someone in jail.

I didn't say anything. Naomi glanced between the two of us before slamming her bong back down on the table, the bowl popped out spilling ashes on the table.

"Fucking fine, but if he's not in jail in a week I'm gonna go kill him myself.

She stormed out of the room, shoving Brian into the wall as she passed by him. He didn't do anything, just avoided her eye contact until she had slammed the front door behind her.

"Where do you think she's going?

"Probably her girlfriend's, I replied.

"Do you think she'll forgive me?

"Yeah, she's just pissed you're friend's with assholes. You came clean, she'll move on.

"What's his address, Brian?

"I've never ratted before …

"You won't, I'm gonna.

"Still, I don't know what's gonna happen?

"Hey, I said getting him to look right at me. "He's gonna do something fucked up, you're not betraying whatever code you got, you're possibly saving someone's life. You're not like him so you gotta do what's right. Now what's his address?

He nodded and sat down next to the table. He pulled his phone out and the wrote down the address on a piece of paper we had laying on our living room table. "I checked his snap location, he should be there right now.

"Thanks, man.

He handed it to me before walking into his room and closing the door.

* * *

Brian decided to move all of the drugs out of our apartment, in case that hillbilly fuck decided to talk to the police. He didn't tell me where and I didn't ask. Then he gave me a burner phone he had for "work and I drove out of the city. I didn't know how tracking worked on these things, but I was feeling paranoid and I felt there was no harm in distancing myself. The car ride was slow and I felt myself looking over my shoulder the entire way to the woods.

I called 911 and told them Billy's address, that he sold drugs, and that word on the street was that he had a Pact. They tried to get more out of me, but I hung up and tossed the phone out the window before heading back home. In lieu of a voice modulator I simply tried talking in a deep voice combined with some unknown accent. I'm sure I sounded retarded, but I didn't really care.

When I got home I told Brian it was done by shouting through his door. He replied, "okay and I walked away I grabbed a beer from the fridge and took a heavy bong rip before heading to my room. I curled up into the corner of my bed and started watching cartoons on my laptop. The sun wasn't down yet, but I just wanted to sleep, I just wanted to be nothingness. I just wanted it all to go away.

Chapter 9

Billy was arrested that night. Brian told me that he had heard it from his plug, apparently everyone was wondering how he got caught. We even saw a brief snippet on the nightly news, we didn't have cable so we had to google it. Supposedly he had tried selling pot to an undercover cop posing as a twenty year old a couple years ago, so that was the main theory. He hadn't talked the first time, but now he was facing life. Not a life sentence, but now it just took five years to do the trick.

Everyone was slowing down on business so Brian ended up earning himself a little vacation. Doing little to calm his nerves, he spent the entire time pacing and almost immediately giving up on any task or form of entertainment. He seemed sober (for Brain's standards) the entire time, which was reassuring for Naomi and me. Last thing we needed was for him to get blacked out and have some sort of episode or something.

Naomi seemed to have moved on, but I felt that some part of her was still unnerved about the whole thing, not that I wasn't either. The good news was that he told us and we were able to fix the issue, but most people aren't as brazen as Billy. On the other hand, the idea that he could just be selling around with someone who had a pact and enough brain cells to keep quiet undoubtedly made both of us a little anxious. Brian too, however, had different reasons to be afraid of people with pacts.

Everyone started quieting down when someone on the inside talked to him. Apparently the cops were grilling him pretty hard about the notion of him having a pact and he admitted that he may not have been the most discretionary. Probably got his ass kicked for that. Brian said that rumors start circulating around, but most of them didn't merit much attention. Everyone Brian sold with calmed down, convinced themselves that he was just a dumbass, and that he was gonna eat the charge because he was "a good guy.

It took a while for Brian's edge to dissipate into himself.

* * *

"Hey, man, you missed the turn, you gotta take a right on Polk, I said.

"No, I know, I just gotta make a stop first. Then we'll go to In-N-Out, Brian replied.

"Alright, whatever, man, I said as I went back to my phone. I scrolled aimlessly through Twitter, getting my daily brief of news from the trending section. I saw another bill that was passed into law; that got me heated. I scrolled through a series of jokes mocking right wing pundits and felt my anger slowly dissolve.

"Wait, hold on. Where exactly are we going?

"What do you mean? Brian replied.

"Like, are we going down to the gas station to pick up beer or are you dragging me to some shady shit?

"Nah, man, I'm just dropping off an eight ball.

"What the fuck? That's shady shit.

"Dude, it's just an eight ball.

"You know Naomi and I said no dealing at the house and don't do it when we're with you. Why are you playing with me like this?

"Look, she just hit me up and I've dealt to her before. She's a college kid, it's no biggie.

"Context isn't the issue, I made it very clear that I didn't want to be a part of your job.

"Look, I won't do it again and I'll buy your lunch. It'll take a minute, just be chill.

"Fine, whatever, I replied. "But you better not be doing this shit again.

Brian didn't reply and I went back to my phone. I closed Twitter and flipped through my apps in search of stimulation. I settled on a cheap game before putting my phone away, bored a minute later. I stared out the window as snow covered trees drifted by while the mountains stayed in place, looming over the town. The signs and names of the stores began coming more trendy as we neared the campus. I assumed the food and items were the same quality as anywhere else, just hidden behind fancier storefronts. I questioned whether this was my dad's opinions seeping out through me, but I let the thoughts slip away and out of focus. Eventually Brian pulled into an expensive looking apartment complex.

"She lives here, I'll be back in a second. Just stay here.

"What made you think that I wanted to come up? I asked.

Brian gave me a sarcastic thumbs-up and exited the car and I watched him walk into the building. In the meantime, I switched the AUX over to my phone. Low tempo house music started playing through Brian's Honda Accord. Not really the car you'd expect from a drug dealer, but Brian said he googled the most popular car of the year to avoid attention. He was halfway through a two year lease and so far he hadn't been busted, so props to the critical thinking of drug dealers.

I reluctantly opened one of the various dating apps on my phone. I scrolled through, more for entertainment than anything else, although admittedly my heart rate spiked whenever I made a match. Just a couple days of chitchat, at the best, before everything just ends up falling off the radar. I kept looking up toward the dorm entrance, waiting for Brian to come back out. It occurred to me that I didn't actually know how much product was kept in his car and with no one else in the car I'd probably be the one taking the fall.

After a couple of minutes Brian finally emerged from the dorm, waving emphatically with some girl in tow. I flipped him off and went back to my phone, not exactly enamored by the idea of meeting one of his clients. When I looked back up and they were closer, I was able to recognize the girl he was with.

"Oh, fuck me, I muttered to myself.

Behind Brian blowing smoke from a vape was Tierra, bundled up in a large jacket with a college beanie covering most of her blonde curls. When she saw me she was momentarily taken aback before she began laughing. Brian gave her a quizzical look as she hopped into the back seat. Brian came in and started the car again, momentarily causing the music to skip.

"Hey Danny, this is Tierra, she's gonna grab a quick bite with us. Tierra this is Danny.

"Hello, Danny, very nice to meet you, Tierra said while sticking her hand out between the seats. "I want you to know that this is just a study-buddy because obviously, nothing is more important than my future.

"Very nice to meet you as well, I said returning her tone. "I'm glad I changed your mind. I was worried I was just being a drunk asshole—glad to know I successfully rehabilitated you.

She rolled her eyes at my attempt at an apology and dropped back into her seat.

"Wait, do you know each other? Brian asked.

"We actually do, Tierra replied, beating me to it. "Danny here was offering to be my sponsor which is ironic considering that he's apparently a drug dealer.

"I'm not a drug dealer. I live with a drug dealer and I wasn't told that Brian was working today or else I wouldn't be in the car.

"Oh, wow, aren't you just a saint.

"Look, I get it, I was being a jackass, I had no right to tell you how to live your life. I'm sorry.

"Apology accepted, she said slightly more sincerely.

"Wait. Was she that girl you got into a fight with when you and Naomi ditched me?

"Naomi told you about that?

"Oooh, what'd she say about me?

"That Danny blew his shot with a cute girl cause he got on a moral high horse, again.

"Well, that sums it up pretty nicely I'd say, Tierra said.

"Agreed, I replied. "Let's get some burgers.

* * *

In-N-Out had a pretty backed up drive thru which was no real surprise. Good, cheap food and for some reason you didn't feel like a piece of shit even though you were getting fast food. Tierra was ribbing me for not having premium as another ad popped up over the stereo; I switched the volume down. A game I played was trying to turn down the volume before I could figure out what they were advertising, just another small way for me to fight back against corporate America. Unfort_-nately, it was for the Navy and they open up with what they're selling so I never stood a chance.

"So what you don't like the Navy? Tierra asked.

"No, he just does that for any ads.

"Although, I'm not really a fan of the Navy.

"More of an Army guy? Tierra asked.

"Nah, if I got drafted might as well go for the Marines. Although knowing me, I'd go to the Army after I failed boot camp.

"If you got drafted?

"I'm under 30 so I'm first priority. If World War III breaks out no way I'm dodging the draft for more than a couple months

"You could dodge it.

"Trust me, my odds are slim and I've never been lucky.

"Alright, what about you, Tim?

He stifled a giggle at my reaction. Took me a second to remember that he told people a fake name when on the job. As if the cops weren't going to have any more information than the name to go off of.

"Well, Tim would end up joining the Coast Guard or something, wouldn't you?

"Uh no, fuck that, Brian replied. "We both know that the both of us would be hauling ass for Canada.

"Yeah, except that both of us have rap sheets. They're not gonna let us in.

"They're hippies up there, they won't give a shit, Brian said.

"A, yes they will. B, I feel like that's racist.

"Wait, said Tierra cutting in. "You've both been arrested?

"DUI, I said pointing at myself. "Possession, pointing at Brian.

"Wow, what a couple of badasses.

"Mine is cool, his is just being an idiot, Brian said, pointing back at me.

"Agreed, I said.

"So did you guys go to jail? she asked.

"I just had to go to a bunch of AA meetings and my insurance rates fucking rose exponentially; he got off scot-free.

"Cop forgot to read me my Miranda rights, said Brian with a shit-eating grin. "God bless Detective Eisman, the beautiful moron.

"Are you serious?

"Some serious bullshit, he always gets lucky like that.

"Eh, you should pray more; you never know.

Tierra scoffed.

When we got to the front of the line both Brian and I got our usual burgers and fries along with milkshakes and Tierra just got a burger without onions, probably cause Brian was buying. Brian parked outside a Home Depot and we casually ate inside the car, my music still playing lightly through the speakers.

"Who are you playing right now? Tierra asked.

"Uh, *Like a Tattoo* by Owen Vonn, I said while glancing at my phone.

"Okay, fuck yeah. I love that song.

"Yeah, he's actually playing next month. If you wanna come I'll bring some Molly, Brian added.

"Okay, down.

I reluctantly reached for my phone and pulled up Brian's number. His contact still said Brian (Spanish) from back when I first got his number. I shot him a quick text and put my phone down. He looked away from Tierra who was still talking about her last rave and checked his phone. He gave me a glance and smirked before putting his phone away.

"Wait, Danny, do you buy drugs off of Tim?

"Yeah, why?

"Cause that coke we did was pretty top notch, not that Tim's coke usually isn't as good …

"Hey, c'mon, Brian protested. "I promise I got the best shit north of Phoenix.

"Yeah, he really does, I reassured her. "I just get the stuff before he cuts it.

"Bro.

"Wait, is he serious? You asshole! What have I been snorting?

"I add a little caffeine to it, calm down.

"That's reassuring.

"Hey, I interjected. "I'm just kidding, he does use a test kit He is selling clean shit.

This was partially true. Naomi had bought him a test kit off Amazon that remained unopened for a month. After Naomi stumbled onto the unopened box, the two of them got into an argument. Since then she had been testing his batches for him. She hadn't found any fentanyl, although she had found small traces of meth more than once. Brian claimed he had brought this up to his supplier and flushed it, which calmed Naomi down. If I was a betting man though I would guess that he simply sold the tainted product to interested parties and never mentioned it to his supplier.

"Well, I don't care, Tierra protested. "Either give me the real shit or cut the price or something. I don't want any of your stepped-on shit.

"'Stepped-on shit?' Brian repeated. "What have you been watching, *The Wire*?

"Stop stalling.

"Okay, fine. You're now in the inner circle. I hope you're *both* happy.

"I mean I'm relatively happy, I said.

Tierra smiled smugly and sat back down in her seat.

The three of us then preceded to talk about raves again which turned into a conversation about psychedelics until Brian began the drive back to the campus. When we got back to Tierra's dorm I gave her some bullshit about how I needed her number for the rave and she gave it to me with an eyeroll.

* * *

"So her, huh?

It took me a second to respond to Brian's question (accusation?) because I was mouth-fucking the last of my strawberry milkshake.

"Look, I like her, I said as I wiped pink cream off my chin. "Whenever have I ever asked you to back off on a chick?

"It's fine, I'm interested in her roommate anyways.

"Okay, perfect.

"Also, what the fuck was that about?

"What was about? I said with fake innocence.

"Telling her I cut the shit, I don't show up to your job and tell the customers that you spit in their microwaved food.

"I don't spit in anyone's food, that's just bad karma.

"I don't give a fuck; don't fuck with my work, man.

"Okay, fine, I replied. "I was just trying to make her laugh.

"Well, next time don't throw me under the bus. Alright?

"Look, what do you care if one person knows?

"This is what I do, he said with a glare. "Believe it or not, people talk.

"Okay, you're right. I was just still irritated cause I didn't wanna get dragged around while you're working.

"Make up whatever excuse man, I don't care.

"Alright, I'm sorry. I won't pull that shit again.

"Okay, good.

* * *

We mostly stayed silent until we got home. Brian parked his car and snagged his backpack out of the backseat. We entered our apartment to Naomi drawing in the living room. I turned on the TV and sat next to her while Brian went to his room. He came out and headed for the door.

"Where you going? Naomi asked.

"Work.

"Then why did you take the drugs out of your car? I asked. Brian paused at the door before turning to face us.

"Fine, I'm going to prison.

Naomi stopped drawing and glanced at him inquisitively. I was slightly more disturbed by the notion.

"You know, if you call the cops and sign a confession, they'll pick you up and take you there themselves, I said.

"Why are you going to prison? Naomi interrupted me.

"To visit Billy. I always promised I would if he promised he'd visit me.

"Don't say anything man, if he— I started.

"I'm not retarded. I'm gonna vow to find whoever put him in there and just keep him company, that's all.

"You know he deserves to be there for life for what he's done, right? Naomi said.

"Obviously, but still.

"Okay. Be safe, Naomi said.

"For real be careful, I added.

"Sure, Brian replied with a slam of the door.

Naomi sat up and dropped her indigo pencil. "Well, that was unexpected.

"Are you okay with that? I asked.

"Sure. Are you not?

"You literally weren't talking to him for almost a whole week, now he's visiting the guy and you don't give a shit?

"I was mad that he hadn't called the cops on that piece of shit and that he lashed out at us. He apologized and got him arrested, if he wants to visit him out of some sense of pity or honor code I don't care.

"You are genuinely out of your mind.

"Whatever. You still not drinking?

I shrugged.

"Not on work days, so kinda, yeah, I replied.

"You working tomorrow?

"Nope. Wanna grab a handle?

"Absolutely, she said beaming.

Chapter 10

I had about ten minutes before I clocked out of my job and handed my tables over. I had shown up an hour early to cover a coworker and now I had been there for almost eight hours and was more or less exhausted. I worked at a cheap Mexican restaurant with all of the charm of a resort on the edge of the border. Mostly white people and a decor that was reminiscent of a 1950's Hollywood director's idea of Mexico. It was hard to complain though, I got good tips and my uniform covered my numbers so nobody was peaking and trying to judge me.

The table I was currently serving was a sweet old pair of Fascists who couldn't stay away from politics. In all fairness, I had known plenty of younger couples who couldn't resist dragging strangers through the mud in casual conversation, these two just happened to be older. I had ignored most of their comments and smiled politely at all their little jokes. Crazy how twenty (probably ten) percent of their bill and the threat of unemployment and suddenly I was the most affable person in the world. Sure I had rung up their coffee as decaf but they hardly seem to notice as they rambled away on the state of the world.

They actually had the audacity to ask my numbers to which I had replied that I was raised a Gnostic, a simple get around that wasn't directly a lie.

"Well, I'm sure God has given you a high number. You seem like a nice enough young man.

I chuckled and thanked them as I scooped up their plates and tried to push for dessert. It was always curious to me how these customers seemed to think that my beliefs lined up perfectly with theirs. You'd think that after years of waiters unanimously agreeing with them they'd pick up on it. Maybe they didn't care or ignorance was simply bliss. Regardless, I got a "fun look into their life.

I got to the back and ran into Katie in the kitchen. She had a tangle of curly hair in a ponytail and her work uniform was always impeccably washed. She was actually a true gnostic through and through, never got her numbers. We had briefly talked about it in the two months that I had worked here, but for the most part we just shit talked customers.

"Hey, you off at seven?

"Yeah, why? I replied.

"Me and Jason are going to Lumberyard's across the street for a drink. You wanna come?

"For sure. Just gotta finish up God's true believers and that couple sitting on their check.

"Oh, were they astonished with your tragic end?

"Katie, I'm a man of God, I said over-dramatically, putting my hand across my chest. "I never got my numbers, but I'm so sick of those rapscallions with their weeds and mollies.

"You really are a saint, she said with a dry tone. "I'm glad you found your people.

"Uh-huh, I replied as I grabbed our dessert menu and went back out onto the floor.

As I turned the corner I saw an unexpected face. I dropped off the menu and cut off the customer's question with an apology and beelined to the bar.

"Luke?

He turned around and he immediately lit up. He went in for a quick bro hug kinda thing. "No way, how have you been, man?

"Good, just the same old shit, working as a waiter to pay the bills. You?

"Just got an easy job selling insurance. I'm studying for the LSAT and I wanted to take a year off.

"Good for you, man. That's law school, right?

"Yeah, good money. And I think I'll enjoy it.

"Well, hurry up, and you could represent Naomi and me sometime.

"In my first year I'm gonna only try to take winning cases so I'll have to pass on that.

I laughed and I grabbed a seat next to him after looking around to make sure my manager was off the floor.

"You here with anyone? I asked

"Some college buddies are gonna be here in a minute, just waiting. What have you been doing since I've last seen you?

"I'm staying in an apartment with Brian and Naomi right now. Just waiting tables now and watching the clock tick.

"Brian's an asshole.

"Well, yeah, but he's surprisingly a decent friend, plus he does the dishes.

Luke chuckled. "So how's Naomi?

"Great, I'm sure she'd love to see ya sometime.

"Oh yeah.

"Well, she's got a girlfriend, so probably not what you're thinking.

"Oh, fuck you, he laughed trying to hide his disappointment.

"Look, just come over sometime. We haven't seen you in a minute and I can definitely find a night when Brian's not over.

"Yeah, bet. Luke's smile faded and he took a swig of his beer. He sorta stared off, looking away.

"Everything good?

"Yeah, man, he replied. "I just heard you were rolling pretty heavy, it worries me you know.

"Dude, anyone who is a shorter hears that shit all the time. You know how rumors are?

"Yeah, but you're the only shorter I've heard that's overdosed on coke.

"What? You've only heard of one shorter OD'ing?

"Okay. I heard you OD'd. You doing good?

"Who told you I OD'd?

"I don't know, man, just someone.

"Well. I didn't. Okay? I mean do I fuck around with drugs, but I'm not some fucking dumbass who's borderline suicidal.

"Look I'm just worried. Okay?

"No, man, I hate how everyone just assumes the worst about me just cause 'God hates me' or whatever.

"Don't get political.

"Dude, it's my life. How can I not get worked up about it?

"You're right, he said putting his hands up defensively. "I just heard shit, I clearly overreacted. My bad.

"It's all good, man, I said.

I glanced around over my shoulder looking again for my manager or a needy patron. Nothing; place was dead. As my mind conjured up potential urgencies, Luke broke my train of thought.

"Do you remember when we TP'd Liz's house after she broke up with you in high school? he asked, breaking the silence.

"Oh my god, honestly. Fuck her. She had that shit coming.

"Right? She definitely knew it was us though.

"No shit, I laughed. "It was the same week.

We reminisced about our adolescence for a couple minutes

or so before I saw my manager come in from his smoke break. I made a hidden shooting myself in the head motion before returning back to my tables. When I clocked out later I told him to text me and he said he would and then we went o_r separate ways. This time he stayed behind though.

Chapter 11

We were driving tonight. I was against it, but it was Brian's turn to pay for the Uber and he decided to drive instead. Naomi said it was his choice, but she made him take all the drugs out of the car in case we got pulled over. Brian claimed that only people with bad karma get pulled over for DUIs. I told him driving drunk was how you get bad karma, but he just scoffed at me.

So I sat in the backseat, sucking on a guava vape and an IPA, as we made our way to Flagstaff's best (and only) strip joint known as the Honey Bee. The rumor is that they named it something innocent so they could get their building permits before they revealed it to the public as a nude bar. I found this doubtful, but several of the strippers had repeated this nonsequitur and it has been part of the legend ever since.

I was drinking my beer out of a thermos in case the fuzz pulled us over, Brian was drinking out of a Sprite bottle that he had mixed gin into. Naomi was cautiously sipping from it, waiting for her edibles to kick in. Best to not get too drunk in case you get too high as well. Of course we had all been doing blow which is the only reason that going to the strip club seemed like a good idea. Anyone who goes to the strip club sober should seek professional help. Even if you work at the strip club, if you're going sober, talk to a specialist.

We got to the strip club and as per usual Pete was standing outside. Pete was about 6 foot, 8 and went through approximately two packs of American Spirits a day. This stench was mixed with an expensive cologne, which when combined properly, actually smelled halfway nice. Pete also was briefly institutionalized and now took enough antipsychotics, stimulants, and antidepressants to tame a gorilla. While on the job he has sent twelve grown adults to the hospital for disputes in the parking lot. The strippers had a running bet pool on how many he would hospitalize each year. Naomi had actually been allowed to toss in this year. Apparently she had put a hundred on four cause Pete was a scary motherfucker.

He was also Brian's drug connect to the strippers. Brian had for years said he wouldn't supply other drug dealers (because that's how you get caught), but being the head honcho at the strip club was too tempting of an offer. Plus, as part of Pete's deal with his doctors and judge, he has an alcohol collar on his ankle and a weekly drug test, not only to verify that he wasn't doing illegal drugs, but more importantly he wasn't straying from his doctor's prescribed medication. A guarantee of being sober, a deep disdain for rats and weak men, and a connection to some of the sleaziest girls Northern Arizona had to offer had earned Pete a job as Brian's drug connect to the strip club. Quite frankly, Brian would've probably sold directly to the strippers himself if the owner hadn't gotten involved, but it was better this way.

We had stopped at the gas station for a complimentary pack of menthol American Spirits for Pete. As we approached the front of club Brian tossed the pack towards Pete who caught it and stuffed it in his back pocket. Pete was staring intently at a pudgy man in the parking lot who was fumbling his keys.

"All good in the hood? Naomi asked him.

"No, that man scared Charlie last week. I told her that if he even stared at me funny I would break his nose and break his teeth like sticks. I want to bite off his ear.

"Well you know the deal, boss man, said Brian. "If you get arrested you could potentially lose your job with me and the Honey Bee, so try not to stir up too much trouble.

"Don't listen to him, I'm betting on high numbers this year. So if you think you need to teach him a lesson you do what you do best, okay, Pete?

Pete grunted and flicked his cigarette at the man. Without breaking eye contact, he pulled out another cigarette and lit it up in between his teeth.

Meanwhile, Brian gave Naomi a playful shove and shook his head.

"Don't listen to her, Pete, Brian said. "We're a team, you and I. As part of our team, I say don't assault strangers cause that's bad for business.

Pete grunted again and took a deep drag from his cigarette.

"Hey Danny.

"Hey Pete, how you been?

"My therapist says I am making strides and that she's proud of me.

"That's great, man, I replied.

"Yeah, she's nice. Charlie misses you.

"Well that's why we stopped by to say hi. Thanks for looking out for her, big guy,

Pete grunted.

"Can I have some of your Sprite? he asked.

"Nah, it's got bubbly in it, but I'll get some inside and bring it out to ya, okay?

Pete nodded and gave Brian a fist bump and with that we made our way in.

The inside of the Honey Bee was a sticky yellow that was surprisingly well lit for a strip club. The walls were adorned with playful insects and dripping honey. The disco balls had been specifically designed to be in hexagons so the lights flashed make-believe honeycombs that danced along the walls. The stage, jutting from the back with the runway, split off in the middle of the room to two smaller stages with bright aluminum poles. One of the gentlemen visiting the club had apparently taken a stripper back for a lap dance; only the Native American dancer Bashful Beaver was dancing alone on the stage. Her real name was Mildred and the stage name had been given to her by the club owner. She found the name racist and was actively protesting it, but her job was more important to her, so she danced to it. She was a sweetheart and she deserved better.

The wall left of the entrance had a bar with bikinied bartenders and the far right wall was lined in private rooms. The girls at the bar were what the owner considered "projects." Essentially they wanted a job, but not stripping. They also felt that Brian was a bad influence on the girls and Pete so they held a deep disdain for our little group. Therefore, we brought our own alcohol and left them alone. Whenever I was forced to buy drinks from them I always made sure to tip extra heavy to win them over, but it was pointless.

As we took a seat at one of the tables, Mildred saw us and lit up. She hopped off the stage and embraced Naomi in a massive hug. She was topless and only wearing fur pants, which also seemed racist. Her hair was in two braids that swung as she ran. She was skinny, but not too skinny, with amazing tits and a smile that lit up the room, but you never saw it at this place. The dozen other patrons who bothered to show up on a Wednesday booed as she hopped off the stage, but Mildred didn't care. Again, she was too good for this place.

She sat down at our table and waved at the bartenders. One of the girls started coming over.

"Oh my god, Naomi, you look gorgeous."

"I'm in a crop top and shorts. Are you high?"

"YES! Mildred leaned in real close to Naomi's face, "I took three points of Pete's new Molly and I feel absolutely amazing. I just pretend all these creeps aren't here and I feel incredible when I dance. I've refused private dances all night because I feel like it would ruin my high and I just feel like I'm gushing. Are you high?"

"Just edibles and coke, Naomi said.

"Oh that's a bummer. Do you want Molly?"

"No, I'm fine, but I'm sure one of these gentleman will take it.

Before Brian could reply I chimed in.

"Brian's driving, hand the points this way."

Mildred took two points out of her pocket and slid them to me. I quickly took them and flushed them down with beer. I set an alarm for forty minutes so I wouldn't be completely caught off guard. When I looked up the bartender was standing over Brian and glaring at him.

"Can we get one bottle of champagne? Brian asked.

"Sure, the bartender said as she turned and walked back to the bar.

"I don't know what her deal is, she's a Gemini. I think the moon's in retrograde right now. Anyways, Annie's been asking about you, Naomi. I think she, like, likes you. She's so cute. I really think you should ask her out, she's sweet too. Plus you both have awesome boobies.

Mildred reached out and grabbed Naomi's breasts.

"Whoa, Mildred murmured.

Naomi carefully pulled Mildred's hands from her chest as a man in the back whistled.

"Hey honey, wanna get a private room and talk in there? Naomi asked.

"Oh my God, yes! Mildred replied. "Will you tell Sophia to bring two champagne glasses to our room? she asked me.

"Sure, I replied. "Just be gentle with Naomi, okay?

Mildred covered her giggle with her fingers and took Naomi's wrist with her free hand. She led Naomi away with a bounce in her step. Naomi turned around just to roll her eyes.

"Holy shit, she should not be doing three points, Brian said when she was out of earshot.

"Be nice, I replied. "Drugs are meant to be fun; she's having fun.

"Uh-huh, Brian said.

Two more strippers rushed out. One I recognized as Sarah, her dancer name was Krystal, and the other girl was new. They both strutted down the stage to whistles but had to wipe the polesdown with rags. They tried to look sexy doing it, but it was just too practical to be appealing. Sarah was spinning with her hands free, breasts bouncing, but the other girl was struggling. I imagine that had a certain appeal to some of the patrons, fresh meat this.

"You know Naomi told me that most of these girls are lesbians, I said to Brian.

"Don't repeat that to me. That's like telling a six year old there's no Santa.

"Well what do you want to talk about?

Brian turned to look me dead in the eyes.

"I don't want to talk to you. I want to look at tits and pay girls to dance on me with cocaine.

I raised both my hands in defeat and we went back to watching the show. I found myself wishing that they had better music in strip clubs. They always played to the lowest common denominator at this club. Just shitty pop and overplayed hip-hop. I wanted electro funk. I wanted punk rock. I wanted blues country. Just something with some soul and a reason to exist. None of this off-brand shit.

"Hey Brian, cool if I borrow your bullet and head to the bathroom? I asked.

"Just do it here, Pete's not gonna toss you out, he said.

"Only an asshole flaunts power. Just let me do it in private.

Brian rolled his eyes and we slapped hands across the table. When I stood up I had a silver vial in my hand. I excused myself to the restroom and found a stall. While usually bullets are designed to be shaken with a trap door that deposits a small dash of coke to the surface for snorting, I felt like a fucking rip. I screwed off the top and poured out a line on the top of the toilet tank. Usually I would spring for the baby-changing station, but for some strange reason strip joints didn't have those. I cut the coke into a fat fucking line with a grocery store gift card and railed it up my nose. It burned and I felt the bitter taste of the drip in the back of my throat. I smiled and hunched over against the wall. I sat there for a minute or two before I stood up and made my way back to the table where Brian and I were seated.

Brian was talking to a girl in pink underwear and a blonde bob cut that went only to her shoulders. The girl had black makeup on, heavy mascara, and when I approached the table she smirked. She walked over and played her hand directly on my crotch and whispered into my ear.

"Your friend offered me a whole lot cash if I could manage

to make you cum. How about it, big boy?

I rolled my eyes and took her hand off my crotch.

"Lead the way, mademoiselle."

She grabbed my hand and started toward the stage. I tossed the vial back to Brian and followed her. We passed the private rooms and made our way through the velvet curtains into the back of the house. I saw a few customers exchange glances as we peeled behind the permitted zones.

The back of house had cement walls vandalized in chalk highlighted by brightly burning fluorescent lights. The dancer pulled off her wig to reveal a buzz cut and threw the wig at the wall. I let go of her hand and continued to follow her through the bleak hallway.

"I would never have tried to give you an erection if I thought it was longer than three inches, the dancer said to me.

"Oh, it's four and a half at least. Don't be a cunt, Charlie.

Charlie smirked.

We walked into the dressing room where one girl was snorting a line, another was drinking vodka straight form the bottle, and two in the corner were making out. One of the girls gasped and threw her hands over her chest.

"Oh, calm down, Samantha, Danny has seen you naked a thousand times.

"I don't care, don't bring citizens back here.

Charlie narrowed her eyes, "You're a whore, act like one.

The girl flipped us both off with both hands as Charlie went to her locker. One of the two girls making out looked over and winked at me before putting her hand down her girlfriends panties. I looked away and made my way over to Charlie.

"Do you bring me back here to make them uncomfortable or to make me uncomfortable? I asked.

"Oh, stop acting like a bitch."

Charlie was putting on jeans and zipping up a puffer jacket. As I turned around Annie was standing there.

"Hey Annabel.

"Only my grandmother calls me that.

"Sorry. Annie. Force of habit. How you doin'?

"Good. Are you just here with Brian or …

"Naomi is here, I said with a smile. "She's been asking about you. I think Mildred is talking to her privately about what a great mother you would make.

"Oh, no one would want me to be their mother, Annie said with a blush.

"Well I doubt that's true. How about you find Naomi and do your best to get her pregnant, okay?

"Stop it, Annie said. "God know I've tried a thousand times to get that girl pregnant.

"Well, try again, she's always happier the next day. I wish you'd come over sometime, I'd love to see Naomi smile while sober.

"Hey, lover boy. Charlie said while smacking the back of my head. "Stop flirting for your girl and come share a cigarette with me.

"Duty calls, I said as I walked away with Charlie. She pushed open the emergency exit and we were standing in two feet of snow in the back of the parking lot.

"I'm gonna go get a pack of cigarettes from Pete, Charlie said.

"Give him a blow job for me.

Charlie flipped me off as she rounded the corner of the club.

Charlie was an interesting soul. She had sworn that she had

slept with a thousand guys and never had an orgasm. She then said she had slept with two thousand girls and never had an orgasm. She tried masturbating, but had never gotten into it. She eventually decided that she wasn't sexually attracted to anyone and that she no longer had any interest in looking for a significant other, she only cared about friendships. Through bizarre circumstances we had become friends and she told me that she valued that above anything else. I trusted her and held her in significant regard.

Charlie came back with the pack of cigarettes we had recently bought Pete. She already was holding one in her lips and offering the box outstretched to me. I took one as Charlie lit her own with a Snoopy Zippo lighter. She passed the flame to me and I lit up as well. I took a deep inhale and felt the smoke burn at the back of my throat as I let a short exhale out of my nose. The smoke gently left my nostrils and disappeared into the frosty air.

"So I'm guessing you don't have a girlfriend? Charlie asked

"I'm at a strip club. Obviously no.

"You'd be surprised, most of these men have wives.

"Well I hold myself to a higher standard, I replied.

"Right just alcohol and designer drugs for you.

"Is that harming anyone?

"Yes, obviously yes. It's harming you, she said.

"Lost causes don't count.

"Oh stop being a pussy and get clean already.

"Whatever, how's Culinary School going? I asked trying to change the subject.

"Got accepted into one in New York City. I've saved up enough money dancing that I can actually afford to go now.

"Congrats I said as I brought her in for a slight side hug.

"You should be proud of yourself.

"Eh, they accept most people. It's just a massive wait list.

"When do you leave? I asked.

"Seven months, in August.

"That's great, I'll miss you.

"Yeah, you'll have to convince some other dumb chick to come out here and shoot the shit with you while your room-mates get blue balls.

"How about instead I just give you a call?

"Sure, but I'm never visiting this podunk town again, she said. "Once I'm out, I'm out for good. If you wanna share a cigarette you'll have to fly to the Big Apple.

"I hear they have great stand-up in New York.

"Is that what you want to talk about? Professional jackasses?

"No, I suppose not, I said.

"Then what's up? Charlie replied.

"I don't think I have much time left.

"'Til?

"Until I'm dead, Charlie.

"Don't you have like four years left?

"Something like that, but I don't think I'm gonna make it, I said.

"Oh stop being a pussy, Danny.

"I'm not. I've had two overdoses and all my attempts to get sober have failed spectacularly.

"Then try again, she said.

"If only it was that simple.

"It is, she said.

"How'd you get sober? I asked.

"I had goals. You need goals.

"Like what?

"Mine was to stop being a stripper, she said.

"That's helpful, I said sarcastically.

"It should be. You're a whore too.

"I mean I don't get laid all that—

"No, you fucking idiot, Charlie said as she massaged the bridge of her nose. "You're a whore to your base desires. You wanna be happy, you drink a beer. You wanna party, you snort a line. You want to sleep, you take a xanie. You need to learn how to live without being a bitch to your simplest whims. Get sober, go for a jog, eat food that didn't come from a microwave. Learn to live. That's your goal. Stop being a whore.

"I don't know if I have it in me, I replied.

"You'd be dead if you didn't.

"Maybe I'm just lucky.

"No such thing, Charlie said as she flicked her cigarette into the snow. "My break is over.

Go cry on someone else's shoulder.

She banged on the door and someone opened it.

Charlie gave me the finger and disappeared inside.

I stood still and took a deep inhale of my cigarette. I stared into the forest and lost myself in thought. The trees were thick and bountiful. I hoped for an elk or some forest critter to come out and peek at me, but nothing emerged.

Alone with my freaking-out brain, I started feeling intense and overheated. I was confused until my alarm went off. That's right, I had taken those two points, they must be kicking in now. I thought about banging on the door to be let inside, but figured without my escort I would probably be told to fuck off. I trudged around the side of the building, my thoughts were going a million miles per hour. *Is this a heart attack? Is this a panic attack? Fuck, place your hand on the wall. Breathe. Breathe.*

Okay, walk forward.

I came around the corner and Pete was standing there smoking a cigarette. I sat down on the floor next to him. I asked him for a cigarette and a light. He obliged. I continued to sit on the ground as I sucked the cigarette down to the filter. After it was done I dropped it on the ground. I pulled off my shoe and used it to put out the cigarette so I didn't have to stand up. While I was putting the shoe back on Pete asked me if I was high. I told him that I was fucking blitzed. He nodded and pulled out another cigarette. He offered me another and I shook my head. The first fifteen minutes were always rough. I just needed to breathe. Just breathe.

I made my way standing up and headed toward the door. I needed to talk to Brian. I opened the door and was accosted by bright lights. The lights shone like diamonds and I couldn't see much. I made my way toward the table where Brian and I were sitting earlier and sat down. It was someone completely different than Brian. He looked at me strangely and I immediately got up and left. I looked around and saw Naomi waving me over. She asked how I was doing and I said I was way too high. I told her I was low-key freaking out. She took my hand under the table and held it gently while stroking the back of my palm with her thumb. She told me to relax and breathe. *Relax and breathe. Relax and breathe.*

Charlie came over. She was on the stage. She started whispering to Naomi. She looked back over at me and told me to hang in there and that she cared about me. I told her that I cared about her too. Then I went back to breathing. I held my eyes closed to shut out the light. *Everything would be okay. Everything would be okay.*

Naomi took a Waymo back with me twenty minutes later.

I was up for hours listening to my favorite music. I was better at home.

I felt like hell the next day.

Chapter 12

I should not have remembered this day. Not because I was fucked up or chemicals I had ingested altered my ability to process and retain memories. Not even the multiple mental illnesses that make memory difficult a psychiatrist told me I had, who even knows if he was right. Just a quack my parents had me see after I dropped out of my single semester at community college. I should not have remembered that day because it was a Tuesday. I was going to eat, serve a bunch of pretentious customers at my job, come home, get stoned, watch a TV show Twitter convinced me was actually good, and then go to bed. Like a normal fucking Tuesday. Instead we got robbed.

Brian was asleep, Naomi had the day off so she was in the living room with me. I was eating breakfast courtesy of the fast food joint across the street and drinking free coffee that my apartment complex offers (most likely funded by the deposits they were keeping on trumped up charges). Naomi was rattling on about how the Mets were actually New York's real team (her parents were from Astoria) and I was listening mostly to goad her on, when the door opened.

Two men walked in wearing dirty hoodies, jeans, and Halloween masks—one some type of ghost hoodie that covered his whole head and the other was wearing a giant plastic Luigi face with his blonde hair sticking out behind it. It looked like he had donned the mask and then stood in front of a leaf blower for an hour. They would have looked exceptionally retarded if it wasn't for the weapons. Luigi was holding some type of pistol and the taller one with the ghost face was holding an aluminum bat that still had a sticker from Dick's on it. Luigi was a little shorter than me with some girth behind him and his buddy was lankier, but tall enough that I wouldn't wanna fight an unarmed version of him.

Luigi shut the door behind them and locked the door. The tall one held the bat as if he was gonna hit us even though we were across the room. I slowly put my hands up and I looked over to see Naomi do the same, less fearful though, more irritated as if she hadn't grasped the situation. Luigi talked first.

"Hey, we're here to rob you. I'm not a violent person so nobody is gonna get hurt as long as nobody does any stupid shit, like fighting or lying. I'm fucking serious!

His friend tried to look menacing as Luigi waved the gun in our general area. "Where are the drugs and money?

"Like Acvil? Naomi said in a dry tone.

I shot her a what the fuck glance before the Batboy jumped in, "Do you wanna fucking die? he yelled.

Luigi shushed him before looking back a us. He had a smear of makeup on the side of his neck clearly trying to cover up some surely tasteful tattoo.

"No, we know Brian Johnson lives here. We know he sells drugs. We want his fucking drugs.

"And his fucking money!

The ghost-mask guy was almost bouncing now as he waved his bat back and forth, as he got closer I could see his eyes were rimmed red. His breathing caused the mask to be sucked in repeatedly, creating a wet spot over a white smile plastered on his face. The bat always stayed behind his back, waiting for a swing that would hopefully never come.

"He's asleep in his room, do you want me to grab him? I asked.

"Does he have any weapons in there? Luigi asked.

"No. I lied, I genuinely didn't know.

"Alright, *you're* gonna walk me in there and *you're* gonna wake him up. *You're* gonna talk to him and make sure he's not trying to pull any shit.

He pointed the gun at me each time he stressed "you.

"Sure.

"Come over here; walk backward. He said pointing at a point on the floor near him. "You stay there, honey. My buddy is gonna make sure you don't do anything stupid.

I could hear Naomi mutter "gross as I slowly got up and made my way backward through the room. Ghost mask kept me at a distance, constantly shifting focus between me and Naomi. I stopped at the point in the floor and kept my hands raised.

"Which room is his?

I pointed.

"Good. Now go open the door.

As I started walking over I felt the tip of the pistol graze my back. My minimal knowledge of gun safety and action movies told me that this was unwise of him, but fortunately for Luigi I was not suicidal (enough, apparently) and didn't care enough about Brian's drug stash to do shit about it. I reached Brian's door and slowly pushed it in.

Brian's room was cold, he had left the window open and the shades slowly drifted in the breeze. The walls were barren, except for a small poster that he had gotten from a smoke shop and a large painting on a stool leaning against the wall. The painting showed a small boat floating toward a tropical island, a stark contrast to the rest of the decor. His desk in the corner was littered with souvenirs and trash in no particular order, a murky mirror lying on top of them near the edge. A couple of clothes were scattered through the apartment, but most laid in an overflowing basket near his closet. Brian's bed was toward the back wall, with him and a brunette girl in it. Brian was still asleep, the girl was leaning against the wall on her phone, staring at us with paralyzed eyes. She had long brunette hair and was fairly attractive despite looking slightly anorexic and exhausted. I think I had met her before, but couldn't be sure.

"Hey, Lily, right?

She shook her head without breaking contact, "It's Kat.

"Right. We're being robbed. Do not call the police. Just wake Brian up. Seriously do not call the police.

She dropped her phone and immediately started shaking Brian, who grumbled and turned over. He looked up and followed Kat's eyes to me and Luigi.

"Ah, fuck me.

He threw over the sheets to reveal himself just wearing gym shorts and slid his feet onto the ground.

"Look, take whatever you want. All I have is my laptop and phone in this room.

"We're here for the drugs, dumbass.

I grimaced as his voice boomed over my shoulders, stinging a bit.

"Yeah, I know. Brian said with a shrug. "Why'd you open the doors? he asked looking at me.

"They barged in! I was eating breakfast.

"Well, how many times have I said to keep the doors locked?

"Are you fucking serious?! I shouted back. "What do people say about not bringing your work home with you, dumbass?

"Hey! Luigi shouted again. "Everyone, shut up! Now walk outside and sit down. Then me and Brian will come back for a scavenger hunt.

"I haven't reupped in a couple of weeks, but whatever.

"Yeah, we'll see about that.

Brian got up and took Kat's hand to lead her with him. She kept close behind him as we began walking out. She was wearing underwear and one of Brian's shirts that said YOUNG vertically, starting at the bottom. As we reentered the room we saw Naomi glaring at Batboy who had finally let the bat hang at his ankles. When he saw us he immediately backed up and held it back in an unorthodox swinging position again. We all sat together on the couch.

"Now you, said Luigi with Brian at gunpoint. "We're gonna find the drugs, then everyone is gonna leave happily.

Brian got up and started heading to his room again with Luigi following him. "I told you I don't have shit, but, whatever.

We were left alone in the room with Batboy. Naomi got off her chair and sat down next to Kat, putting a supportive arm over her shoulder. I wasn't sure if they had met before, but Kat leaned into it and started softly crying. This gave Batboy a slight chuckle who remained in the middle of the room, pacing with his eyes fixed on us, he kept swinging his bat in a choppy arch like he wanted us to try and pull some shit. Naomi shot him another glare which I'm sure he only enjoyed. I leaned back into the sofa, trying to get comfortable as we waited.

The waiting was the worst part. I'd never been robbed before, but I had police search my house which is remarkably similar. Obviously the cops aren't gonna bash my head in with a baseball bat, but honestly I'd rather spend a week in the hospital than a year in jail. Either way you're just waiting helplessly hoping that shit doesn't go sideways.

A couple minutes in we started hearing some shouting from Brian's room. Something about him hiding or lying.

"Yo, what's going on in there?

"Mind your business! Batboy yelled back at me.

Brian came back out with a bloody nose being led by Luigi again. The blood was dripping off his chin and onto his chest turning his torso into abstract art. There were long smears down his arms where he had tried to wipe the blood away before apparently giving up.

"You okay? Naomi asked.

"I'm fine.

"Not for long, Luigi retorted. "Someone doesn't want to tell us the passcode for his safe. So instead of beating the living shit out of everyone here, I would like it if someone just told me the fucking combo.

He looked at the group of us sitting on the couch. Naomi stared right back at him as Kat pulled her closer. I chose to look down, just hoping not to piss anyone off.

"I don't know his combination; it's not my safe, Naomi said.

"I didn't even know he had a safe, honestly, I said putting my hands up. It was actually the truth.

Luigi looked over at Kat. "How about you, buttercup? You got any ideas?

Kat shook her head no and Luigi sighed beneath the mask but before he could say anything Batboy yelled, "Goddamn it and smashed the TV with his bat. Shards of glass shot out and the Xbox home screen was replaced with a blue streak flashing sporadically, where there was still glass.

"Does it look like we're playing?! I will kill all of you moth-erfuckers.

"Hey! Luigi shouted. "Keep it quiet or else the neighbors are gonna come running. What did we talk about?"

Batboy nodded, fuming and swinging his bat beneath him, little cuts appearing all over his arms.

"Alright, now we're gonna…

"Brian, tell him the fucking combination man! What the fuck?! I yelled.

"I don't know it! It's my parents safe!

Luigi smacked him in the back of the head with the butt of the gun, an action I couldn't help but understand. Brian shot him a glare and bit on his tongue. Batboy couldn't stop scanning the room, searching for God knows what. He looked like he needed a xanie, a nap, and a lobotomy.

"So here's the deal, Luigi commanded. "If I shoot any of you, cops are gonna get called, we're gonna have to run, and whoever I don't manage to kill gets to explain to the cops all the drugs.

Kat sobbed, Naomi pulled her closer.

"I'm gonna keep the gun at Brian's head and my friend is gonna start beating people until we get what we want. Any volunteers?

I looked at both Naomi and Kat. At this moment, I felt like I truly didn't give two shits about Kat, but I'm sure Naomi did. She wouldn't let Kat get hit, at least not first. I figured I'd probably do better getting hit than Naomi. A rogue thought told me that was sexist, but I ignored it, and raised my hand. I would chuckle at the intrusive thought while remembering this days later, the fucking irony of it.

"Get up.

I stood up and walked into the center of the living room. I reminded myself I need to clip my nails as I felt them dig into my palms. Batboy was mocking me, practicing his swing. He wanted this. I could hear Naomi yelling something in the background; I didn't know who it was directed at.

"Lift your hands up above your head, Luigi said.

I lifted them up.

"Okay, fine. I'll tell you! shouted Brian. "Just leave my friends alone.

"Wait, Luigi said.

Batboy stared at me, then reluctantly let the bat drop to his side. "Keep your hands on your head, he said to me. "What is the combo?

"69, 42, 0.

"Hit him.

I looked at Luigi and made an attempt to plead my case before my left side was smashed by the bat. I fell into an end table, knocking over a lava lamp on my way to the ground. My entire body was pulsing with my ribs at the epicenter. I fought for breath as I pushed myself back against the wall, momentarily placing my hand on the fallen lava lamp for balance. I wouldn't realize it burned me 'til about an hour later.

"That was the right code!

"I believe you, but that's what you get for wasting our fucking time. Now M— Luigi caught himself before continuing. "I'm going to have my associate open the safe.

Batboy nodded and went into the other room. We waited in silence. Naomi was glaring, but I was unsure if it was at Brian or Luigi, possibly both. I made my breaths come deep and slow, it didn't seem to help, but I wanted to feel control of something. There was that bubble of panic rising, the idea that I might explode. The recurring thought, that if I panicked something bad would happen, only increased my panic, just a broken cycle that stretched my anxiety to its limits.

The idea of blood pumping into my lungs flashed in my head. It was impossible to understand if that's even possible. With no frame of reference for internal bleeding I couldn't articulate the pain, I touched the bruise lightly and a sense of nausea overcame me.

"Danny, are you okay?

"Fuck off, man, I replied to Brian.

"Did I say talk?

"Can I get him some ice? Naomi asked.

"When we leave, I don't give a shit. Until then sit and shut up.

"I hope your true love has genital herpes.

Kat hit Naomi in the shoulder and shook her head. Luigi just stared back at her without saying anything.

"Why isn't the code working? we heard Batboy yell. Luigi pushed the gun harder into Brian's back.

"Turn the safe lock left three full times to reset it, then turn it right, left, right. It's the right code, Brian said. "Your buddy is a genius, huh? Brian muttered.

Luigi gave a slight snort. Eventually Batboy came back into the room with a duffel bag slouched over his shoulder.

"Oh, his safe was plenty full.

"Haven't reupped huh? I could hear Luigi's smirk in his voice.

Brian remained silent, staring at the ground. Luigi shoved him forward and kept the gun pointed on him. Brian reluctantly sat down on the table. Batboy moved toward the door and Luigi followed him walking backward, gun still flashing.

"Hey, if any of you think you see us in public, don't say shit cause we'll fucking kill you.

And, with that, Luigi and his associate were gone.

* * *

Naomi ran and locked the door. I got up and sat on the couch. Brian was pacing in circles, his fingers kept tapping the side of his leg like he was keeping beat to some song. To his credit he eventually noticed Kat crying on the couch and went over to comfort her. Naomi went from the door to the kitchen and pulled a bag of french fries from the fridge. She sat down across from me and grabbed my hand.

"Pull off your shirt, she said.

"I think peas are better for ice, Kat said.

"Do we look like we eat peas? Naomi asked.

I lifted my shirt using only my right arm. I winced when part of the shirt caught the underneath of my armpit, shifting my left ribcage. The bruise was still growing, a massive purple mass shifting as more blood pumped into it. I groaned as Naomi placed the fries against it, she let go as I held it myself. The cold stung.

With that Naomi walked over to Brian and Kat.

"Brian, get up.

"Why?

"Cause when I hit you I don't want to hit Kat.

Brian reluctantly got up, covering his face like a boxer. Naomi stood still, possibly waiting for him to lower his arms before she kicked him in the balls. Brian groaned and fell back into the couch.

"Oh, fuck! Was that necessary?

"Yes, you fucking asshole! Wanna ask Danny if he feels like you deserved it?

"Naomi, relax. Let's just figure things out first, I said trying to stand, but I sat back down. "See.

"Shut up, man. I'm gonna kick you in the balls, too, once I'm feeling better.

"Can someone drive me home? Kat interrupted.

"No, we gotta wait 'til the cops show up, Brian said.

"What?

"Yeah, fucking *what*, Brian? I said, agreeing with Naomi.

"Look, we gotta take you to the hospital. We move out everything inconspicuous and expensive, then we tell the cops we were robbed and get insurance money.

"Oh, yeah, that's brilliant, I said. "We just got robbed, let's commit insurance fraud!

"Why not? It makes sense.

"No. It doesn't, countered Naomi.

"Look, I'm out some serious shit, okay? Brian said, his voice cracking.

I'd never heard his voice crack before, I'm sure getting hit in the balls didn't help, but still.

"There's no cameras on the back gate. We move out all the shit, drive it to my buddies house; after the cops leave we move it back. Easy Peasy.

"Man, we're looking at a couple grand, I said. "I've been arrested before and I'd rather not risk it for the money.

"Look, we need that money.

"*You* need that money, said Naomi. "*We* need to not get arrested.

"Yeah, can't you just tell the cops you lost that gun? I said.

"No, it's a friend's. We shouldn't mention that.

"What's that got to do with anything? Naomi asked

"It means he had an unregistered gun in our apartment. What the fuck, Brian?

"I've got a fuck-ton of drugs in my room constantly. Are

you really gonna give me shit about breaking one more law?

I shrugged; a certain fucked-up logic, I suppose.

"Look, how about I drive Kat home and you guys think about it. Okay? Brian said.

"Are your roommates home? I asked Kat.

"They should be.

I nodded. Brian and Kat got up and started heading for the door. Brian walked with a bit of stagger and I saw some amusement in Naomi's eyes. Kat ran back into her room and grabbed her purse; she held it close to her chest.

Before they left Brian said, "Just think about it.

I pushed myself up with a wheeze, I could feel my ribs ache at the slightest pressure. "What are you doing?

"I'm getting a beer, I replied. "You need one?

"Yeah ... What do we have?

I opened the fridge to see an assortment of half a dozen cheap beers. "Rolling Rock, Coors, an IPA.

"You take the IPA, I don't mind Coors.

I grabbed 'em out of the fridge and began to walk back to the couch. I was about to toss the can to Naomi, but thought better of it and set it on the table in front of her. The can popped and I watched the bubbles foam out before slowly fizzing away. The sweet bitterness of the beer felt right, comforting as I held it in my mouth before swallowing.

"You know Ben Franklin said beer was proof God wanted men to be happy.

"Didn't he have a syphilis? Naomi asked.

"Yup, not sure why we have a guy who had a sex-disease that makes you go crazy on our hundred-dollar bill.

"He'd probably be a good hang.

"Probably, but that's what I thought about Brian, too.

"You can't afford a new TV either can you?

"No, I spent my last couple bucks on that tattoo last week, remember? I said motioning to the San Francisco Mountains captured on my arm.

"Right ... So we're really gonna do this, huh?

"I don't know what *we* shit you're talking about. I can't move shit right now.

Naomi put her beer down on the table and went into her room. I could hear her say something along the lines of "fuck my life.

I sipped my beer and tried to relax as I closed my eyes.

Chapter 13

"So they robbed you an hour ago and you're calling now? the cop asked.

"Yeah, we were just so scared, Naomi replied.

We had asked Naomi to play up the scared victim card in front of the cops. She said that was sexist and we agreed, but we didn't want any suspicions. Eventually she agreed after we admitted that she was tougher than both of us. I don't know if that's entirely true, but we let her have it. So now she was crying like a girl who was trying to get out of a speeding ticket in front of the two apathetic cops.

Felt weird staging a robbery even though a robbery had actually happened. In a weird way I felt like we deserved the money, fuck the corporation and all. Sure we were doing illegal shit, but what happened crossed a line.

An ambulance was on the way for me. If I wasn't still on my parents insurance I would've just told the cops to get my statement at the hospital, but it's pretty much the same for me now. I'll just try to get my dad back for the copay, he won't accept anything but I'll still try to pay out of pride. I don't know if I'd try if I thought he'd take my money. I hope I would.

I had called my dad after the cops told us they were on the way. The call made me feel guilty, just cause of the way it made me feel. It felt nice talking to my parents and for once they weren't mad at me. I hadn't realized how much I had missed my relationship with them. Like when I used to come home from school and we would talk about just some bland stuff. Now it's all about how I need to get my life together. Even when we talk about anything else, it's just sitting in the corner, a black cloud in our relationship just poisoning every interaction, making something pretty feel forced.

So now their sympathy was hiding that black cloud from us, but it'd be back. Once the pain was gone, it'd be back.

The second cop was getting tired of hearing Naomi and approached me still on the couch. He was in his mid-thirties and surprisingly in relatively good shape. He seemed irritated that we had waited, as if we were trying to make his life difficult. I was lying down on the couch at the cops' orders, but forced myself to slightly sit up.

"So, the assailant struck you in the chest after your roommate, Brian, refused to initially give up the combination to the safe?

"Yeah, I figured it was either me or Naomi, right?

The cop grunted and looked back down at his notes. "Can I ask why you felt you needed a safe in this apartment?

He looked around our apartment, assessing the Craigslist couch and the tattered posters hanging on the wall.

"In case we got robbed.

"Why were you under the presumption that you were going to get robbed?

"Well, we were, weren't we?

"Yes, it seems that you were. He looked up from his notebook at me, inspecting me for something like he was practicing to make detective.

"I'd suggest selling the safe and finding new roommates.

"Thanks, I'll consider it.

"Uh-huh, can I ask what your numbers are?

"Why?

"For my report. It could give us input for statistics and possibly help us solve who did this to you.

"Can't you just get fingerprints or a piece of hair or something?

"Look, this isn't a murder scene, okay? It's not like TV where a bunch of nerds solve everything. Can you just give me your numbers?

"It just doesn't seem relevant.

"Are you the police officer?

The other cop looked up from Naomi and came over.

"I'll talk to this one, you just go outside and wait for the ambulance. The second cop grunted and walked out of our apartment.

"Thanks.

"Look, it can't hurt to comply.

"I know.

The cop sighed.

"Anything you noticed that your roommates may have missed?

"I think one of them had a neck tattoo and the other one's name starts with an M—the first guy said it and caught himself.

"I knew about the second part, but the tattoo thing is helpful. Anything else?

"One of them was definitely high, I'd guess some kind of upper. I wouldn't know though, I quickly added.

"Don't worry, I'm not putting you on trial. Just sit tight.

The cop walked back over to Naomi and I leaned back into the couch. Brian was sitting on the other side of the room. He kept cracking his knuckles and looking around sporadically. I wondered if he was high, but I hoped he had better sense than that. The first cop went over and said some something to him. He answered, but seemed to talk too much. Then the EMTs burst in. The first cop pointed to me and I stood up, revealing the purple bruise on my side.

I laid back on the couch and the paramedics inspected me before asking if I needed a stretcher. I told them no and they walked me out. I waved to Naomi and Brian as we began walking into the parking lot. The ambulance was sitting in the middle of the parking lot, the lights flashing silently. A couple of my neighbors were watching, most likely passing judgement. I ignored them as the paramedics helped me get up into the back. One of the paramedics gave me a slight shot and I felt my breath get slower, my pain numbing. The light dizziness started and I made a mental note to ask the medic what he gave me later.

I felt the vehicle move as I tried to convince myself I would be okay.

* * *

The drugs had worn off at the hospital, I was lying in the bed watching TV trying not to move. My name had been red-tagged when I got to the emergency room so they switched me over to less addictive painkillers. Now my only relief was from Advil and a sitcom that made me embarrassed for humanity.

I always thought that'd be fun to write for a living, to produce something that would be around after I wasn't. Not that I'd actually be remembered, everyone and everything is forgotten in time. At this point my thoughts and ideas were probably so decrepit and far from mainstream I'd be lucky to find anyone at all willing to read anything I touched.

My thoughts of self-pity were broken by Naomi and Brian entering the room. Brian still seemed shaken, but Naomi seemed more like her normal self.

"Hey, bud, how you doing? Brian asked.

"Ah, my name got flagged so I got pulled off morphine and they stuck me on Advil.

"Oh, fuck that, Naomi chimed in.

"Yeah, but I'll be good in a little bit. They said I'm not as beat as they'd expect for taking a slugger to the side.

"I got a buddy who's got painkillers if you want some, I can bring them here to you, Brian said.

"No, I'm okay. Thanks though.

Brian nodded and they both took seats in the chairs next to the bed.

"Hey, if it's any consolation, I told Tierra you were in the hospital after protecting Naomi.

"Okay, protection is a stretch, but what girl are we talking about? Naomi asked sitting up.

"Just a girl I met at a bar who enjoys buying the finer things from 'Tim' here.

"Which girl?

"Out of two I'm guessing.

"Fuck off, Brian, the one with blonde curly hair.

"The girl you managed to piss off completely?

"Yup, so how much money are we gonna get from the insurance company? I asked trying to move on.

"Whatever, but probably a couple thousand, Naomi said. "Honestly I think I'm the only one who's gonna come out of this looking good.

"We haven't talked about what we're doing with the money. Brian said. "I mean besides the TV, I'm the only one who got robbed.

Naomi and I shared a glance before I spoke.

"Are you serious? We got robbed cause of your dumbass and if you had just told them the code in the fucking first place I wouldn't be in the hospital! Why in the world would you get it all?

"Cause I need the money. I had a ton of shit in there. Am I just supposed to tell my plug tough shit and do me a solid?

"I don't know, figure it out! I realized I was yelling. "We're splitting the money three ways. We all got robbed. We're sharing it.

"Can we talk about this later? Naomi broke through. "I'm the one who got the policy, the check comes in my name, we're splitting it. End of discussion.

"I'm just saying ...

"Well, don't, Naomi said defiantly.

Brian nodded again before standing up. He was nearly out of the room before he stopped and turned around.

"Look, guys, it's my fault I know. I'm sorry, Danny, I fucked up. I'm gonna make it right. I just gotta go call my supplier real fast.

"Hey, until you know who those guys are, you might wanna be careful who you talk to, I replied.

He nodded again as if he hadn't considered this and then shut the door behind him.

"How you holding up? I asked Naomi.

"Oh, I'm fine, just putting up with him trying to subtly ask for money the entire ride over.

"God, what's gotten into him? This feels like a whole new level for him.

"I don't know; he seems scared.

"Shit, really?

"Yeah, like really. I don't wanna give him the money on

principle, but after I pay for the TV I'm gonna probably give him the rest as payback for drugs I've owed him.

"Shit, I owe probably more than you, we'll split the TV and I'll throw him the rest. We have to move though.

"Yeah, Naomi sighed. "I don't think I could do that again. When is our lease up?

"Four months or so.

"Alright, we'll give him the money on the loan as long as he agrees to pay for moving. Work for you?

Naomi was interrupted by my family bursting in. My mom and dad immediately came to my side while my sister waited farther back. Naomi gave my sister a supportive hug.

"God, are you okay?! my mom asked.

"Yeah, Mom, I'm gonna be fine. Just a little roughed up.

"The doctor said you fractured some ribs!

"Well, yeah, but those heal. Honestly, I'm okay.

"Yeah, you look like a million bucks, my dad scoffed. "I'm glad you're okay though.

"Thanks, Dad, I appreciate it.

The small talk continued, the usual elephants in the room were bottled up by the incident.

Same way every moronic president gets a massive spike in the approval rating after a disaster only to watch it slowly dwindle down to decimal points. Sympathy has a short lease. Naomi excused herself and I watched my sister follow her out. My sister came back in after a couple of minutes.

"So, people often are a little frightened returning to burgled homes. Do you wanna stay with us for a couple days? my mom asked.

"He was robbed not burgled, my dad said with a scoff.

"Sure, that sounds really nice, I replied ignoring my dad.

"Okay, good, my mom said relieved.

* * *

"So I talked to Naomi, my sister said.

"Yeah, she's the best right?

"Considering she's not a drug dealer, she's definitely my favorite of your roommates.

My shoulders sagged and I pushed my head farther back into the cheap pillows. "Fuck.

"So, do you do this shit to piss us off or does it just come naturally to you?

"'Naturally, I suppose.

"Glad we made a breakthrough. Now you wanna fight those instincts and get your shit together?

Chapter 14

"Dad, I don't wanna talk to him.

"He's a family friend, my mom said. "He wants to check up on you. We're not trying to convert you, just be polite for a couple minutes.

"You owe us, my dad added.

"Okay, fine. You're right.

My parents eventually left and I laid in the stiff hospital bed. I had a remote this time and I spent a minute or two channel surfing before I gave up. My left side ached still and Advil doesn't have the same dampening effect as my preferred pain killers, so I just tried to keep myself occupied on my phone. Unfortunately you can only refresh Instagram so many times, so I laid back and tried to sleep with little luck.

Brian had come by earlier in the day to sneak me a few shooters. I lightly chastised him, but accepted regardless. I was sipping on some rum when Patrick came in. He glanced at it hesitantly as I shoved it underneath the sheet. He was a tall skinny man of about fifty or so; he radiated the energy of your favorite uncle. He wore a dark golf shirt, plain pants, and on his right wrist he wore a leather bracelet that extended from his wrist to his elbow. The bracelet had a small lock in the center.

The bracelet was a paragon of the mental strength of a born-again Gnostic. Essentially they chose to ignore their numbers in favor of a more preferable life. So even though they knew their numbers, they chose to forget them and live life as if they were completely ignorant. Most of them were devout, kind people. To me it still felt like a cheap trick.

"Lucky I wasn't a doctor, he said as he draped his coat over a chair.

"Aren't you both legally not allowed to tell anyone?

"No, that'd just be the doctors, but I won't   anyways, he said as he settled into the other chair.

I nodded as I tried to relax back into my reclined position. I gripped the mattress tightly underneath the sheets as I did so.

"Sorry, I responded. "I know you came out of your way to come here, I didn't mean to make it awkward.

"It's fine, I've heard everyone's horror stories. I promise I've seen worse. How you feeling?

"Wishing I hadn't lied.

"Who'd you lie too?

"My parents. When I was twenty I told them I was serious about getting sober, they sent me to rehab, and now the doctors won't give me morphine.

"Ah, so you're just upset that the doctors know your little secret.

"I suppose. How's everything going at the church?

"Fine, same as you remembered it I'm sure. A few new faces in the congregation, but mostly the ones you remember. Michael is still the lead preacher and he's doing a mighty fine job if I say so myself.

"It's nice to hear it's growing.

"Yes, the new military bill has some folks being sneaky. If they claim to be Gnostic, the government can't see their numbers either.

"Well, if the draft starts up you'll be seeing my face a lot more often.

"Well, as much as I would enjoy that, you don't seem like the type.

"Are you calling me brave?

"No, he said with a smile. "No, I am not.

"Can you do me a favor? I asked.

"What favor?

"My vape died, I say holding up the blue stick. "Can you toss me the one in my bag?

He sighed and followed my finger before producing a boxed strawberry-guava one from my bag. He walked over and handed me the box before returning to his chair.

"Thank you, I said while opening the box. "Felt embarrassing to ask the nurse.

"I'm sure. You should stop smoking those?

"Why?

"Cigarettes are better.

"You smoke? I asked with a cough.

"No, I gave it up about eight years ago. Although I enjoy a cigar from time to time if I'm honest.

"Funny, I've talked to five doctors since I got here and all of them have seemed to have personally quit cigarettes.

"Smoking's more popular than you'd think.

"Or lying to get me to quit. Think you're gonna pick it up in your last year or so?

"Well, I could be in my last year right now.

"I mean your last possible year.

"I don't think like that anymore.

"I mean, I don't even think I'd be able to forget when my birthday was for example as much as I'd try.

"Do you know why I don't think you'd join the church? he asked.

"Why?

"You have a problem with authority. I don't know how

you'd react, but I am positive that you would not join the church to escape.

"Good to know.

"It *is* good to know, it's important to know yourself. If you were to be completely obedient it would strip you away from your desires and what's best for you, but to ignore everyone else is naive for the opposite reason.

"Fair enough.

"Thank you, and as insolent as you are trying to be, I do believe you to be intelligent.

"Thanks …

"And intelligent people don't continue to destroy their bodies and stay in dangerous situations.

"Right, I said, stifling my urge to be a dick.

"Think on it, I'll always be a phone call away.

Chapter 15

We had moved out of the old apartment three weeks after the robbery. As soon as we put a pen to the lease we hauled our shit out. Only Naomi had officially signed our last lease, so we kept her off the new one and went delinquent on our old place. She only had a couple years left anyways, don't know what she'd want a loan for (or who'd give her one).

The last few months went by predictably, nothing of much interest happened which is a kin to most of life. Routine is settled into, you work, pay bills, get loaded with friends, visit your family and occasionally fight, you keep texting with the girl who isn't your girlfriend but keeps talking to you cause of drugs, you make dumb jokes, you enjoy the sunshine and loath the rain. Days bleed into each other and they bleed into weeks and so forth and so on. As complex as life is to understand, it truly is simple.

I was lying on the living room couch as actors with perfect hair, skin, and teeth were fighting zombies on the TV; five years into the apocalypse had apparently done little for their morning routine. I was eating a bagel slowly to keep last night's rum down. A couple of Advils were trying to fight the good fight against my headache, although they were so far ineffective. Naomi walked in and laughed at the sight of me.

"Yeah, like I've never seen you fucked up before.

"Uh-huh. Guess who called me?

"I don't know, did you get drunk and give your number to some creep again?

"Ha-ha, she replied. "No, Charlotte from the front desk,

apparently they're gonna contact a third party.

"You picked up?

"No, they left a voicemail, obviously.

"Oh, well who cares? What are they gonna do?

"I'm not worried, I was trying to make you laugh.

"Oh, sorry, I said as I made my way off the couch. I left my bagel on the table and headed back to the kitchen with my empty coffee mug. "What are you eating? I asked.

"Lunch, like you should be eating.

"Food is food, I replied while filling up my mug. I headed back to the couch followed by Naomi. She dropped down next to me holding a salad filled with peppers and tomatoes and jazz. I picked up my bagel and nibbled at it.

"What are we watching? Naomi asked.

"It's a zombie show called *Gibberish*. Nothing special, but it's decent popcorn TV. See the chick with the red ponytail?

"Yeah.

"Yeah, well she got bit, but she hasn't told anyone.

"So she's fucked?

"Yup, but instead of telling them she's just panicking and putting everyone else in danger.

"That's pretty human.

"No, it's selfish, she's in denial. She should say her good-byes, drop the mic, then run out in a blaze of glory. Instead she's holding everyone else behind and creating a mess.

"So you have no empathy?

"She's in denial; it's stupid.

As I said this she began throwing up on screen. The camera pans to the lead reeling in shock. "See, now they're all pissed and they're gonna beat her to death.

"Whatever. What'd you do last night?

"You were working and Tierra had a paper, so Brian and I just went to The Monte Lista Lounge, had a couple drinks and came back here. I don't have work today so I figured why not?

"Sounds fun. Have you Venmoed him yet?

I gave her a confused look.

"For rent, she clarified.

"Oh, no, but it's no rush. He told me he's already in the black again.

"Really? Good for him.

"Yup, I mean drugs sell themselves.

"Still it's fast, we should get some of that insurance fraud money back now that he's fine.

"Remind me to bring that up, I wanna buy an Xbox.

"Then buy an Xbox.

"Can't. Brian told me he didn't need my rent and I spent it on tickets to go see *Dauntless* next week.

"What the fuck? I wanna go. Tell me this shit.

"I just did.

"I can't afford that.

"Ask Brian, he owes you.

* * *

Three days later and I pulled at the grass. The condensation on it was cold and gave me chills as I chewed it with my hands. The night was flowing completely through me as I stared off at the faraway stage, lasers ripping through the air as a mechanical man ran on the massive jumbotron behind the DJ. The man felt vaguely familiar, I tried putting a name to the character, the swagger, the confidence, the determination. Then I realized it was me. That thought made me giggle and I laid back in the grass, beams of light dancing above me. I felt the music shaking my body as I wrapped my hands around my chest, smearing green marks across my shirt. I felt my body shake at the drop, an instrument in this festival. I glanced over and saw Naomi talking to Tierra, they were sitting across from each other criss cross applesauce, noses inches apart. Their eyes were locked in and I caught them talking to each other about how beautiful they both were. They were right, they both were beautiful. Like super fucking hot. I caught myself smiling from cheek to cheek and giggled again. I laid my head back and closed my eyes. I'm on a train and I can't get off. Stop. Bad thought. Get up and dance. I pushed myself up and started dancing. Fake confidence is the best confidence. I let my knees drop and my shoulders roll. Forcing smiles actually releases dopamine. Force yourself to smile and you'll be happy. Metaphor for the middle class? No. That's weird, keep dancing. I open my eyes to see Tierra smiling and pointing at me, Naomi is still trying to talk to her. I pull her up by her hand and tell her to dance. She's twirling around singing to the song. Naomi quickly follows us both and begins jamming out as well. I look for Brian or Tim as he's known tonight. Does Tierra know Tim is a fake name. That's super annoying. Wait, where is Tim? Brian. I do a 360 and don't see him, just kids in gym shorts and flamboyant scarves. Girls in spandex with bracelets making sleeves up their arms. I see another guy in a T-shirt and jeans awkwardly holding a beer. I yell at him to dance and he looks at me and laughs. I give him a thumbs-up and turn back to Tierra. She's drinking water and offers me some. It's warm and I don't like it, but I drink some anyways and hand it back. Don't wanna die. I mean I got like a couple years left, but dying now would be counterproductive. That's a weird word choice. Well it would also prove fanatics right and screw them. Well, maybe they mean well. Do they mean well? Fuck it, dance. I look at Tierra who's got her blonde curls in a light ponytail that bounces to the music. She's got glitter splashed onto the right side of her face, her eyes shine brighter though. She's staring at me and laughing. We start dancing to the music in sync with each other. The song is about to drop into the chorus and I tell her to take my hand and we start thrashing our bodies together to the beat. When the final drop landed I stood back to take a breath. Tierra flipped her tiny backpack off her shoulder and began rooting in it. I turned to my side and was elated to see Naomi next to us. I suppose she was there the whole time. I smiled and asked her how she was doing. She didn't hear me and I figured it didn't matter so I turned my attention back to Tierra. She was holding out a pack of gum and I snagged two pieces and shoved them into my mouth. I looked back at the stage and saw the lights flashing over the crowd, it looked as if I was in a space movie, looking at the ceiling lights. When you know the hero is hurt, but he's gonna rally and win. I liked that. A fresh burst of spearmint globbed in my mouth and I went to work on it, the gum holding me to reality and keeping me from shattering my teeth. Tierra was giving fresh gum to Naomi who was shoving her old gum into an empty beer can which I suppose was nice of her. Where was Brian? I kept looking for him. Hanging out with him while he was working was the worst. Coincidentally a guy ran up to me wearing jeans and a band T-shirt and asked if I had coke. I said no and asked if Pepsi was ok. He flipped me off while sarcastically thanking me. I made an exaggerated bow and Naomi started laughing and yelling something in Tierra's ear. She laughed and smiled at me. I felt tingly all over again and I felt my body twitch at the excited nerve receptors. I grabbed her hand and started leading her into the crowd. I bumped into Brian and grabbed him by the shoulders. He turned around and gave me an excited hug. He offered me some coke which he pulled from his pocket. I shook my head and then pointed at the guy who had approached me while tapping my nose. Brian gave me a thumbs-up and began jostling through the crowd toward him. Tierra asked me where he was going and I yelled back, work. We locked eyes and I made my move. Her lips tasted salty and I embraced her. My heart was jumping at a thousand beats a minute and the music matched it pace for pace.

* * *

At five I was still up. Tierra was sleeping, glitter still smeared all over her face. I tried drinking a beer to calm my nerves and send me to sleep, but I only ended up puking up water minutes later. So now I laid in bed waiting. I watched morning come, light slowly filtering in from underneath the curtains. The floor began to softly glow, but I had already given the day to the night.

Chapter 16

"What? I tried whispering it as Tierra was still asleep besides me.

"Danny, is that you? Naomi whispered back.

Why was she whispering? "Yeah it's me, you've called me five times. What's going on?

"Wait, are you in here?

"What? No, Naomi … I heard her place the phone down and was saying something unintelligible.

It was four in the morning and I had woken up at the third phone call, but ignored it 'til the fifth one. Tierra had invited me out for drinks the weekend after the rave, now we were both drunk trying to sleep in her dorm room. I was pressed hard into the wall on Tierra's small bed. The lampposts outside lit half the room in a faint light exposing the walls covered in cheap tapestries and photos hung by colorful pushpins.

"Danny? Naomi said back into the phone.

"Yes, my god, what's going on?

Tierra rolled over and looked at me while readjusting her pillow.

"Me and Brian are on acid. She said that phrase in a tone that was rarely so serious.

"Yeah, I know, Naomi. It sounds like it's working. What's up?

I shrugged at Tierra and made a spinning motion with my finger around my temple. She rolled back over with a chuckle. As she went back down, I laid back as well and let my eyes begin to shut.

"Well, Brian started freaking out and ran out of the apartment and now I'm starting to freak.

"Wait, what? What happened? I said, jolting up.

"I don't know, he was talking about guilt and sins and stuff and then he just said he had to go and I think he meant in a physical sense but it felt more like ...

"Listen stay right where you are, I'm coming!

Tierra had turned back over and was repeatedly mouthing, "what? at me. I hopped over her and landed poorly on the floor. My shoulder hit her roommates empty bed as I tried staggering back to standing. I tossed the phone on to her roommates bed as I began throwing on my clothes. I could faintly here Naomi talking in the background as I spoke to Tierra.

"Brian and Naomi were taking acid, had a bad trip, Brian ran out and now I have to grab Naomi and find him.

"What? Why?

"Because I don't want dumbass getting arrested. I shouted as I threw on my hoodie.

"No! Why were they having a bad trip?

"I don't know. Because drugs are crazy, I said as I grabbed the phone. Naomi was still talking, unaware of my brief departure. I turned the speaker phone on and plopped it on the desk besides me as I tried putting my shoes on.

"... but like we were doing this weird thing with these magnets and it was super fun and then he started talking about how they were like a metaphor and I'm pretty sure he meant simile but anyways he kept going on about how he felt guilty and how he had betrayed us or something ...

At this point I was out of the room and running down the hallway with my laces still hanging from my shoes. I heard the door slam behind me and I noticed that Tierra was following in shorts and a dirty ski jacket, still barefoot as she locked her door behind her. I hesitated before motioning for her to hurry up. I started smashing the elevator button while Tierra caught up with me. Naomi was still rambling so I hit mute to quickly talk.

"Look, Tierra, I need to get Naomi out of there in case any cops show up. Can you pick her up and watch her while I go find the dipshit?

"Will Naomi be okay with just me?

"Yeah, I'm sure she'll be fine. Just convince her that everything is under control and talk about some kinda Zen stuff.

I flipped mute off.

"Yo, Naomi, hold tight, alright!?

Tierra was driving her Lexus down the empty roads while I sat in the passenger seat trying to wrap my head around the situation. Brian's snap location was off as usual, typical paranoia about selling drugs. So essentially I was gonna have to just cruise around our house and hope to bump into him.

"Fuck, I said rubbing the side of my head.

"You good?

"Yeah, I've just got a headache and shit.

"You gonna be good to drive?

"Yeah, what else am I gonna do, get an Uber and tell him I'm looking for my friend on acid? I said laughing.

She didn't laugh. It wasn't that funny in fairness.

We pulled into the gate, the tires crushed the slush underneath them as Tierra reached out and punched in the code. The gate slid open and Tierra pulled up to a curb near my apartment.

"Do you want me to come or ...

"No, go find a parking spot. I'll see you in a second.

I opened the door and the cold air mingled into the car as I hopped out. I closed the door behind me as I heard Tierra drive off to look for an unopened spot. I hauled ass toward my apartment, my sneakers crunching in the snow.

I hoped Naomi was still home. The thought of her leaving hadn't occurred to me until I was actually there. Naomi wandering off into the night looking for Brian seemed almost too plausible for her to be doing anything else. Panic was contagious on drugs, especially the psychedelic shit they were doing. One little comment or observation can slowly fester until obtrusive thoughts envelop your mind. Then next thing you know, both of them would be wandering Flagstaff looking for each other or something else, like lost Eskimos with no clear goal. If Naomi was gone there'd be little chance we'd find both of them anywhere else besides county lockup.

I stopped running as I reached the front door and took a beat to catch my breath before slowly opening the door. Naomi was sitting on the couch, curled into the corner. One of her hands was tightly gripping a pillow, holding it to her chest. Her other hand was holding her phone in which she was face timing someone. She turned and immediately dropped her phone as she stood up. Her eyes were black and her hair was up in a very messy ponytail. She was wearing a tank top emblazoned with a snowboard company and in her left hand she had on some glove with lights at the ends of the fingers that were going off sporadically. She was Richard Nixon's nightmare.

"You're here! I only called you a minute ago.

She quickly hugged me and I returned it briefly before taking a step back. "Okay, thanks. Who were you just calling?

"My sister, she's really mad, but she's in Charlotte so she can't help us.

"Cool, that's fine, I lied. Her sister worked at a church youth camp and was undoubtedly going to give her an earful at some point. "Do you have any idea where Brian ran off to?

"No, but he just left.

"Naomi, you told me that like twenty minutes ago.

"Oh, really? That's bad.

"No, it's gonna be fine, alright?

It was not. I led her to the couch and sat down on the coffee table across from her. There was a great series of things that I wanted to say to her, all of which would be quite unwise right now. She reminded me of a spooked owl, not able to focus on anything and her head constantly swiveling. Her eyes, wide and curious.

"Look, I'm gonna go out and find Brian, I'm just waiting for Tierra to get back so you guys can chill together.

"I wanna help find him, she demanded.

"No, don't worry about him. Just relax, everything is gonna be okay, alright?

I reached out and held her hand, she strengthened her grip and I felt her nails dig into my palm. I tried remaining as calm as possible as I steadied my breath hoping she would follow suit.

"Just be careful, your aura has been really off lately.

"Naomi you're just trippin.

"No, I'm not. Well, I am, but I've been noticing it before tonight. Like you don't smile the way you used to and every time you don't think anyone is looking at you, you always seem tired. Like you're just acting and you don't even wanna be an actor. Like you wanted to be a baker or work in a cubicle. Does anyone want to work in a cubicle? Someone has to want to work in a cubicle.

"Naomi, I'm fine, okay?

"No you're not, none of us are fine and that's okay, I think. I don't know, I'm just worried that you're gonna spiral and then we won't be friends anymore and then I won't be able to help anymore or something. Like, who was that Greek guy who lifted globes?

"Atlas?

"No, those are paper, I mean the guy who like lifted the Earth.

"No, Naomi, his name was Atlas.

"Okay, well, whatever, anyways I never got that story. Like why didn't he ask for help?

"Well, he had to lift the sky, that was his punishment.

"Right, but anyways what I'm saying is that no one ever helped him. He could've asked for help, I don't think he ever did. He just kinda suffered. Ask for help.

She pointed to my chest with her gloved hand and pushed hard. "Wait, how long do batteries last on this thing?

She let go of my hand and started fiddling with the glove. The lights were bouncing off her face as she leaned in closer, illuminating her in a gush of bright colors. I leaned back and put both my hands behind me on the coffee table. I wanted to cry. That wasn't that uncommon, I wanted to cry a lot. I just couldn't. I wanted to fucking purge all of my anger and depression out like one of those weird cleanses celebrities were always doing. Just get rid of everything in my fucking body, start fresh. Even if it was at work or in public or somewhere, just to shed it. Even if meant I was only okay for like an hour, just to shed it again. But you can't force yourself to cry, so it just stayed in, permeating my mind. Maybe Naomi was right, maybe I was just a bad actor who couldn't cry.

"Your eyes are weird, Naomi said.

I laughed, genuinely.

"You should see your eyes, they look like the night sky.

"Cool, her smile faded. "Do you think Brian's fine?

"Yeah. Naomi. He'll be okay. We'll just talk to him tomorrow after I grab him.

She nodded, not reassured. I reached out and held her hand again until Tierra arrived.

She burst in the door and immediately looked at me. I nodded and mouthed, "she's fine. Tierra seemed to take a calming breath and started taking off her boots. I squeezed Naomi's hand tight before letting go.

"Stay here with Tierra alright? I'm gonna be back with Brian in a minute.

"Okay, drive safe and avoid the cops.

I gave her a thumbs-up and ran over to Tierra who was just taking off her coat.

She leaned in close for me to whisper, "Hey, Naomi seems okay. Just keep her distracted. There's beer and vodka in the fridge and just ask Naomi if you wanna smoke. I'll be back in a minute.

"Do you have any yay?

"No, I lied.

"Just be functional in case anything serious happens.

"Don't crash, seriously.

"No worries, I'm good! I yelled as I slammed the apartment door behind me and ran into the parking lot.

Chapter 17

I trudged through the snow and got to my car that was in the back of the parking lot. I immediately turned it on and took that moment to try to call Brian. After an exhausting minute it went to his full inbox and I hung up and sped out of the parking lot. I rolled down my windows figuring maybe I could hear him, but after ten seconds of wind blasting my face I rolled it back up. The night was dark and I kept my brights off to avoid any of Flagstaff's finest that were still out and about. I guessed the best way to find him was how my grampa used to play Battleship, just go row by row and wait for a hit. So I began cruising around the neighborhood, block by fucking block, peering through the window. My grampa would never win, but I felt that was just him being a good grandfather.

He was a proud Gnostic, never understood why anyone would get their numbers. He boasted every day of his life that he was happy to let the universe decide and that ignorance was bliss. He passed uneventfully in his home when I was twelve in April. I got a little tattoo, when I was drunk, with that date to commemorate him. I don't know if it was truly for him or me, but it'll be there on my ribcage for me to ponder 'til I die.

He calmed me down and taught me the importance of Gnosticism when I was ten after we watched a man die in church. He was up and singing two rows in front of us when he suddenly dropped, as if someone had turned off a switch and he fell limp to the ground. My grandfather used to be an army medic so he immediately ran over and I naively followed him. He didn't bother checking for his pulse because he noticed his dates on his inner arm. They had never been there before, but now they had appeared in a light blue light, almost dancing. I watched until some woman grabbed me and quietly ushered me away. Found out later that the poor bastard was thirty-two.

My grampa said that the man was happier that way, going on peacefully in his life without noticing the Grim Reaper breathing down the side of his neck. He argued that the man lived happier with the knowledge that he would likely live a long and prosperous life and that if he had truly known when his date was he would've thrown it all away. As a twenty-four-year-old driving around at three in the morning looking for a friend having a bad drug trip, I feel like I can probably attest to that.

I couldn't be that though. All I could think about for days after was how he never got to say goodbye. I wrote letters to everyone that I had ever known in case that happened to me, even though I wasn't eighteen and couldn't die unless I was in a freak accident. I felt that I needed to know, so here I was. Driving through the snow, listening to bad music, and praying to God I wouldn't be arrested for my second fucking DUI.

I saw a man standing outside by the sidewalk who seemed about Brian's build and height.

I slammed the brakes and rolled down the window yelling, "Brian! The man turned around and was certainly not Brian. He had a poorly shaven beard and was looking at me hesitantly. A small dog was besides his feet.

"Hey, are you okay?

"Yeah, I'm fine. Just thought you were a friend. Sorry, man.

"You're fine. Do you need help?

"No. Thanks though.

I drove off trying to keep a reasonable pace as I watched him and his small pug watch me go. He halfheartedly waved as his dog began going to the bathroom, not at all dismayed about the events that had just transpired. He maybe could've helped, but things might as well have been made worse. He probably wouldn't call the cops—probably.

I kept circling the neighborhood making my range wider and wider. He had run off about thirty minutes ago, give or take. I figured he'd have to be in a two-mile radius cause I've seen him run on a treadmill before and anything farther than that would be more than generous. It seemed strategically unwise to be simply roaming looking for him, but I wasn't sure where he'd go. Homeless shelters would be closed and none of us actually would even know where they are. He left his wallet and keys, so, no motels and he couldn't get on a bus. His parents moved to Denver and he hardly ever saw them anyways. Even his suppliers lived far enough away he couldn't get there, but that seemed unlikely as well. The last thing I expect anyone would want to do on a bad acid trip was see their bosses, especially if they had a reputation for violence. Brian claimed that it was always self-defense, but I doubted that was true.

I stopped at a red light and quickly texted Tierra if anything notable had happened.

Hopefully not. The light turned green and I turned left and made my way down a larger street. The street was covered in businesses hibernating for the night with a few lit-up fast food joints illuminating the street, offering cheap, fried food to whatever unfortunate souls wandered the world at this hour. I kept my head on a swivel, glancing to both sides looking for my shithead of a roommate. At the same time, I made a point of trying to stay as steady as possible while going just about five miles per hour over the speed limit. It was fucking exhausting.

I stopped at another light preparing to turn left again. Glancing at my phone, Tierra had texted me that nothing much had happened but that she and Naomi were just talking about spirituality or something.

"Well, shit, that's how an acid trip is supposed to go, I muttered to myself.

As I placed my phone down I realized there was a cop that had pulled up next to me. He was a burly man in his late twenties that seemed preoccupied with his computer mounted on his dash. I took a deep breath and tried to look as bored as I could. He didn't even know I was there so there was no reason to panic, which was less helpful than it should've been. Just had to act boring, cops ignored boring people. Cops dismissed boring people. Cops adored boring people. Just be boring.

The light turned green after what felt like an excruciating minute and the officer drove off. It served as another fun reminder that I probably shouldn't be leaving my drugs in my car. I turned left and turned back into another unknown neighborhood. My breath returned back to normal and I turned my music back up. I felt the bass in my chest and despite the situation I still tapped my finger along to the beat. Then suddenly I saw him. I actually fucking saw him. He was sitting on a bench outside a church just staring at the grand entrance. He was wearing a T-shirt, jeans, and an old beanie I remember him having from high school. He must've been freezing, but he didn't show it. He just calmly was sitting staring up at the church. I slowed down and parked on the opposite side of the street. I grabbed a spare dirty hoodie from my backseat and hopped out to meet him.

I approached him slowly, waiting for him to turn around. "Hey, Brian. You okay?

He turned around and half stood up. We made eye contact and he looked haunted, his eyes dark and his face brightly pale. He was illuminated by the church lights and his shadow was long and stretched across the snow. It was as if he was waiting for the morning so he could ask for an exorcism, but exorcisms only work in bibles and that was a long, long time ago. He slowly sat back down and his face seemed to ease up with the recognition of a friend.

"Hey, what are you doing here?

"Looking for you, man. Naomi told me you ran off. Here put this on.

I tossed him the hoodie and he pulled it over himself, rubbing the sides of his arms as if he had just now realized they were cold. I walked around the bench and sat down next to him. I figured there was a time and a place to be mad and that this certainly wasn't it.

"What are *you* doing here?

He looked startled, as if I had somehow broken his train of thought in the last five seconds. "Oh, I just felt that I hadn't been to church in a while and that I should go.

"Yeah, I'm all for that, man, but you know, there's a time and a place right?

"Yeah, I know. He replied. "You know I sell pot and Molly to the preacher's daughter here?

"Yeah, you've told me that.

"That's probably bad karma.

"Probably not great, yeah.

"Do you think that's why I'm gonna die at thirty-four, man?

"No, you just got unlucky. Just like me and Naomi and

every other poor bastard out there who's a shorter.

"I know, but I don't think that's true. I think I'm gonna go to hell.

"Hey, I don't think that's—

"My parents only took us to church like three times a year on holidays, but I always believed in it all. I even secretly made fun of everyone who was gonna die early, like I really believed they deserved it.

"Well, we don't. Okay? That's just what assholes tell themselves so they can feel better about themselves.

"Whatever, it's different for you. You're a Gnostic.

"My parents are, I'm not.

He nodded halfheartedly.

"Still, though, I was a shitty kid, but I always felt like I was good on the inside and that my numbers would show it. Then when I found out my numbers, I think I realized that maybe I was just a bad person, like maybe I'm just broken or something.

"Look, you know I don't believe in any of that predestination shit, but c'mon everyone has a theory and literally no one has proof. You see that? I said pointing at the church. "That's built off a book that no one can even attest to until they die. I promise you you're not a bad person, we're all just trying our best.

"Nah, I was born a fuckup and I'm gonna die a fuckup. I just gotta stop pretending I'm not. See this? He pulled up his sleeve to reveal his numbers. "I don't care whatever you wanna believe in, but there's your proof. I'm rotten to the fucking core.

He took a deep breath and leaned back into the bench. Words didn't come to me so I just joined him by staring at the church. It shone like a beacon through the darkness, daring any building in the neighborhood to try to compare to it. It was beautiful; I hated it anyways though. I hated how it made people think they were better than me and I hated how the both of us seemed to be living proof that it was right. It just made me feel like I was one dimensional; humans are just simply more complicated than that. I knew without it, people would still put me and everyone else in a box when they met us, but the feeling was still soaked into me. Suddenly Brian stood up.

"Can you take me home?

"Yeah, of course bud.

I got up and he followed me across the street to my car. I gave him some ketamine in the car to calm him down, something I learned from EMTs. Ketamine is good for that kinda stuff. I texted Tierra saying we were both fine and that we were coming home.

Chapter 18

I woke up at dawn with the sun beating through the windows. The living room was a mess and empty now. I slowly pushed myself up from the couch. I kicked my shoes off and glanced at my phone to find it was seven-thirty. I tried taking a sip from a glass of water on the table only to cough up vodka and flat Sprite.

"Yeah, cause what else would it be, I mumbled to myself.

I briefly checked in on both Naomi and Brian to make sure they were asleep. Naomi was in bed and Brian was asleep on top of his covers still fully clothed. I made a point to shut their doors quietly as I went back into the common area. I got a glass of actual water from the fridge as I made my way to my room. It somehow managed to be both refreshing and nauseating.

I walked into my room to find Tierra asleep in my bed. She presumably went to bed after I had fallen asleep on the couch. I was probably the first to pass out, but I couldn't remember. I slid off my jeans and carefully got into my bed. I stayed on the edge to not wake her and I slowly fell back asleep.

When I woke again it was around noon. Tierra was gone and I rolled over to make myself more comfortable. Tierra had texted me.

"Hey, had to go to class. Glad everything worked out last night! Had a great time!

Well, at least someone enjoyed themselves I figured. After ten or so minutes on my phone, I got out of bed. Naomi was out in the living room on the couch playing on our Xbox. She yawned and gave me a faint wave.

"Good morning, sunshine.

"Yeah, good morning to you too, I replied. "How are you up?

"Couldn't sleep. I'm just waiting till I feel tired enough to try again. Nothing else to do today anyways.

"Want breakfast?

"I think it's called lunch now, but not hungry. Thanks.

"You should probably get something to eat regardless.

"I know.

I shrugged and made my way to the kitchen. We didn't have any clean pans so I pulled the cleanest one out of the sink and briefly washed it with napkins before putting it on the stove. Not a great look, but I was just making eggs and prepackaged potatoes so it was no biggie.

"How come your girlfriend didn't stick around this morning?

"She's not my girlfriend, and I don't know. She had class or something.

"Uh, yeah, I don't know what she told you this morning, but she didn't look like she should be going to class.

"Well, that's what she texted me.

"She didn't wake you up? Damn, she really isn't your girlfriend.

"Thank you for that.

"Just sayin'. Do you want her to be your girlfriend?

"I don't know, Naomi, I said as I fired up the stove.

"Does she want you to be your boyfriend?

"No.

"Oooohhh, somebody likes her. Have you asked her to be your girlfriend yet? she asked in purposefully high-pitched annoying voice.

"Can we talk about something else?

"Somebody's in love.

"Literally anything else.

"Okay. But I'll be waiting here for when you need advice

"Uh-huh. I dropped a hunk of butter into the pan and watched it slowly melt. The blob transformed itself into a congealed pool with its former self sinking in and becoming something else entirely. The smell hit my nostrils and made me feel queasy. The smell used to remind me of my mom baking when I was a kid. Now it just reminded me of the way it used to make me feel. Any pleasant memory just tainted by the shitshow that was reality.

"Thanks again for getting Brian, Naomi said as she broke my thoughts.

"Oh, yeah, of course. He'd do the same for me, I replied. "Did he say anything weird or off-putting before he left last night?

"Nah, he was having a good time. Talked about fate and sin and stuff, but then I changed the topic and he seemed fine. The last little bit he just got really quiet. Didn't really bother me any. Then he just left without saying anything. I figured he was going for a smoke, but when I looked out on the patio he was gone. That's when I called you.

"Did you say anything that seemed to rub him the wrong way?

"I don't think, would I remember though?

"No, probably not, I said as I poured the potatoes into the pan which responded with a sizzle. "But he went to church, Naomi. Have you ever heard him talk about religion?

"No. She paused her game and came over to the kitchen, moving magazines and a hoodie off a stool-chair to the ground.

"But like none of us do, so …

"True, I responded, "but I also haven't walked to church in the middle of the night for no reason.

"Yeah, but religion is good. Some people kinda need stuff like that.

"No, I completely agree. It's just, you know, the nature of the religion.

"What does that mean? Naomi's eye's narrowed slightly.

"Just you know, numbers being divine punishment and all. I don't think it's a great idea.

"Fuck off.

"What? You don't believe in that anymore.

"So, what, your religion is better? He should suddenly become Gnostic and everything will be perfect.

"I mean, he won't hate himself.

"First off, we're all on drugs, we all hate ourselves! Secondly, it's not like your religion is so much better. They believe that I'm going to hell just because I might fall in love with another woman.

"That's like only a couple verses. Most Gnostics don't even believe that stuff anymore, it isn't the main message.

"What about the bombing of Designated Date Centers, huh?

"Oh, so, now we're terrorists?

"No, cause plenty of religions have nutjobs. My point is plenty of my people don't believe that God hates us cause of our fates, but they follow it anyways. You're always so literal, like you gotta learn to compartmentalize things. Nothing's perfect, stop expecting it to be.

"Look, I said as I began flipping my potatoes. "I just don't want him believing that he's doomed, alright? You used to be pretty big into that. Can you just talk to him?

"Admit your old religion isn't better?

"No religion is better. All of them are unique and appeal to different people. Just please talk to him.

"Fine.

I went back to cooking and she sat at the counter on her phone. I had expected her to go back to playing video games, but she stayed. I secretly enjoyed the company. After a minute or so she spoke again.

"You ever talk to Luke about this shit?

"In high school, and a bit. Why?

"Cause I saw him at church every week and he was as Waterson as hell.

"Yeah, but I never saw him treat me, you, or anyone else like that at all.

"Well there's my point.

"Look, I'm just worried is all, okay?

"Okay.

I pulled the potatoes and slid them onto plates. I dropped plastic forks on the plates, grabbed hot sauce from the fridge and made my way to the table. I put Naomi's plate down and sat next to her.

"Ketchup?

"No, just hot sauce.

Naomi paused the game and made her way to the fridge. "You know ketchup ruins the flavor, I said as I grabbed her remote and secretly changed the sensitivity settings on the game before gently placing it down.

"Ketchup is delicious. Plus they're just potatoes and you're no Anthony Bourdain.

"I'm offended.

"Uh-huh, Naomi replied while sitting back down. "God-damn it, you're literally a child, she said as her character whipped around the screen unfocused and chaotic.

"I can never resist.

"Yeah, whatever.

I began eating slowly, ignoring the nausea brewing in my stomach. Naomi had a bite or two, but mainly remained focused on her game.

"Did I tell you he was talking about my overdose last time I saw him?

"Who?

"Luke.

"Well, haven't you guys already talked about it?

"No, why?

"Cause I texted him when you first overdosed telling him to talk to you. Did he ever hit you up?

"No, I told him that it was just a rumor when I saw him last.

"Oh. Well he knew you were lying.

"Yeah, I put that together Naomi, I said. "He was doing well though, I added.

"Yeah?

"Studying to be a lawyer and all that. He's gonna be super successful.

"Good, I was never worried about him.

"Well, yeah. He's dying at 92. Of course he'd be fine.

"No, even before that. Some people you just don't know. I just hope he's happy.

"What do you mean?

"Some people are successful and not happy. Some are happy and not successful. Mostly everyone else is in the middle. I was worried he just wouldn't find himself.

"No, I think he's fine, Naomi. You're just high."

"Maybe. I don't know. I'm really fucking tired. She put her mostly full plate down and began heading toward her room.

"You happy?

"I think, but I'm not a shrink so, who knows, she said with a shrug. "I'll see you tomorrow.

"Good-night, Naomi.

She gave me a quizzical look before shutting the door to her room. I went back to my room and picked off the little AA chip on my desk. It was a plastic three-month chip that I had earned when I was twenty. It actually still brought me pride, the fact that I had actually been sober for that long just felt like a win. I remembered two weeks after I had gotten drunk despite Naomi's insistence not to. Just started with a beer and then snowballed. Later that night I had flipped the coin to see if I should do coke.

I stopped showing my face at meetings soon after. My sponsor tried calling, but I just texted him sorry. Afterwards, I got plenty of phone calls and texts, but eventually he stopped. You can only speak to a brick wall for so long.

My sponsor had told me part of getting sober was needing direction, but I haven't had that in years. I had gotten *I wander but I am not lost* tattooed on my chest after I fell off the wagon I don't know if it was to mock him or I was trying to prove to myself I was okay.

I tossed the chip back on my desk. It bounced lightly before settling in the middle, where unfortunately I'd see it again. It was my day off so despite yesterday's insistence that I'd go to the gym, I watched cartoons on my laptop while bouncing around on dating apps.

* * *

I heard a door open from my room. I hit mute as two superheroes preceded to beat the living shit out of each other on the screen. Brian's grumble confirmed it was him and I tossed my laptop to the side of my bed. I opened the door to Brian with a beer already in his hand sitting on the couch. I flipped on the TV and sat down next to him.

"Whatcha wanta play?

"I don't know, something not too violent, he replied. "I still kinda got an afterglow going and I don't want anything intense.

I put on an old arcade game which involved cars and a maze. Simple, colorful, distracting, the way video games were meant to be played. Brian picked up a controller and joined.

We played silently for a while, the only sounds were the comical explosions and zips from the screen. Brian seemed purposefully focused.

"You wanna talk? I asked.

"No.

"Okay. Just let me know when you do.

"Why do we have to talk about last night?

"Cause you ran off and fled the house, Brian.

"I was high.

"Great. Promise not to be high again, it won't be a problem, we don't have to talk about it.

"Can we talk about this anytime later? he said after a long pause.

"Sure, man, I'll let you get your head right.

He nodded and we went back to video games.

Chapter 19

"Hey, guys. I got something kinda weird I wanna tell you two, Brian said spoiling the mood. "I think I'm gonna start going to church again.

Naomi glanced at me, not worried per se, just curious.

"Okay, cool, if you want to then you should totally go for it, Naomi said.

"It's not like lame and shit?

"What? I asked looking at Naomi who was similarly confused.

"Nah, I mean sure I got some issues with the teachings, but the core of it is good. Since when do you care what people think about you anyway?

"Bro, nobody wants a drug dealer who's religious.

"Yeah, nobody gives a hot shit what you believe in. No one is finding a new drug dealer because of theological disputes, I responded.

"Yeah, plus you should never feel guilty about being authentically you. Anything you want to pursue that doesn't negatively affect others you should throw yourself into.

"I guess, was all he responded.

"Speaking of churches, I said, "I need you to promise me something.

Brian laughed and nudged Naomi who joined in with a playful smirk.

"Sure, man, what do I need to promise you?

"Promise that if you're having a bad trip, you'll call us so we can pick you up from a church as opposed to county, alright?

"Oh, god. This shit again?

"Dude, you ran out of the house. We never really talked about it. Just say you'll call us if you're in a bad spot.

"I'm not gonna have another episode like that.

Naomi scoffed. "Look at macho man over here, first guy on the planet to figure out drugs.

"Famous last words, my guy, I said to him while pointing at Naomi.

"Since when did you two become such boners about drugs?

"Dude, we're not even telling you not to do drugs. We're just saying don't get yourself killed or something.

"Yeah, we're high right now, Naomi chimed in.

"Whatever, I didn't help you guys move just to get lectured too, Brian said, getting up and heading toward the kitchen half of the room. "Either of you two want a beer?

"Yeah, I said sitting up. "We're not trying to lecture you, man.

"I don't care what you call it, Brian shot back from the kitchen. "It's not like either of you two ever took anyone's advice either.

I looked at Naomi while Brian had his head in the fridge and she mouthed, "drop it to me. So I settled back into the floor and Brian dropped a semi-cold Miller by me.

"Alright, I just think you should slow down.

* * *

We had just been back from the Dauntless rave and I had been the designated driver, so the beer I held in my hand was only my third. Two weeks ago Brian had been the DD and had got hammered, but was convinced he was good to drive because he had snorted some coke. I was able to convince him otherwise only because I offered to call the uber. The afterparty had shifted from the living room to Brian's room in a rather quick few minutes. Not that no one would do coke in the living room, but Brian's girl Erika was only allowed to smoke cigarettes in his room. So we were now doing coke off Brian's desk. Naomi offered me a rolled-up Washington.

"I'm done, man. I haven't touched coke in three weeks, I think I'm done.

"You're just too sober, Tierra teased.

Naomi smiled, she looked me up and down, before chuckling and putting a dollar bill to her nose. She snorted a line off a picture frame on Brian's desk before handing George to Tierra who took the line meant for me.

"More for me, was all Naomi said.

Tierra jumped and made a high-pitched whooping sound before pushing her left nostril shut and inhaling deep while pushing her head back. I was propped against the wall with a pillow behind my back and a beer in my hand. Tierra approached me singing soundlessly along to the electric punk music playing over my speaker. With an over exaggerated groan I stood up and begin singing along and twirling her. Naomi laughed and pointed at the mirror and then to Brian. Brian nodded and Naomi unfurled the dollar, placing it over a rock before hacking away with her driver's license. I may have been too drunk, but the ratatatata's of Naomi's chopping seemed to be in sync with the music as I swayed with Tierra.

Brian was sitting on his bed looking miffed, his collection of dirty clothes to the opposite side of the bed. He pushed off the bed, landing on his knees, before scooting over to his desk. He took a shot up the nose before returning to his bed.

"Thanks for stopping, Danny. Let me know as long as you're being a pussy I might even turn a profit this month.

"Sure thing, let me know when you need me to pick you up from church again.

"Still on that, huh? Want me to roll through every dumb thing you've done on drugs?

"What, you can tease me but I can't tease you?

"Hey, Naomi cut in, "both of you, chill out.

"I'm chill.

"Danny, Tierra said, turning so both her hands were on my chest. "Let it go.

"Fine, whatever.

I let my body fall back into the wall and slide down onto the pillow. I watched Tierra as she went back to dancing. Glitter was delicately adorned across her face in a sideways S fashion, although the glitter was splatter bombed onto her upper thigh. The light shined pink and gold bouncing off her across the wall like a human disco ball. I motioned to Tierra and she laughed, then began repositioning the light to mess with Erika who was the last in our group. She flipped off Tierra and went back to her phone. Erika actually met Brian through business, she makes LSD in her bathroom. Supposedly went to college and took only chemistry for that purpose, but flunked out after a single semester before learning anything useful. The internet was still a thing though so she figured it out.

Tierra plopped down next to her.

"Did I ever tell you about the time I met Danny? she asked her.

"Tierra, can I talk to you now? I blurted out.

"Why? she asked slyly. "Embarrassed you asked for my numbers? He was so weird about it.

"What are your numbers? Erika asked.

"I mean pretty average, but nothing special. Guess who freaked out and told me not to do coke like a degenerate?

"Guilty, but remember that time we snorted the extra Molly in the porter potties at the Big Wild?

"What's your point, that you're a hypocrite? Tierra asked

"Just thought that was a funny story, I replied. "Plus we're going to a punk-rock show next weekend. Erika, you know the band The New York Dolls?

"Wanna know why Brian's being weird? Erika asked.

Tierra looked at me, before looking down as Erika rolled up her sleeve.

"Wait ... is that in four—

"Three days and seventeen hours, Erika said.

"Maybe.

"You pulled out of the machine?

"Yup, just wish that someone else knew how, she said looking at Brian. "But I never got the year, so odds are I'll be fine. Anyone need anything from the kitchen? she asked standing up.

I raised my beer can and shook it in the air. She gave me a wink and headed into the kitchen.

"Are you seriously not wearing a condom? I asked Brian.

"Fuck, man, you saw how much coke she does. Nothing is surviving in her uterus.

"That's intelligent, I replied.

"Wait, Tierra interrupted. "So, every year around this time she goes through ...

"Yup. She'll be having a party next week because she survived another date; she'll be in a much better mood too.

"She's practically bipolar, Brian said. "Every year, the closer she gets, the more rebellious and moody she gets. She probably won't even be snorting coke a month from now.

"Can we not talk about her? She's just in the kitchen.

"Sorry, Naomi, I replied.

"Can I get another line? Tierra asked.

I glanced at Naomi.

"You sure you need another one? Naomi asked. "You're kinda bugging out right now.

"I'm fine.

"Anything else in the snow, boss? I asked.

"Just caffeine, my guy's good, alright?

"Naomi, did you check his package?

"Hey, wanna not be a backseat driver?

"What's going on? Ericka asked tossing me my beer.

"Someone's not into drugs anymore so they're pretending to be all righteous, Brian explained.

"I just asked Naomi if she'd checked the package.

All eyes went over to Naomi who was in an office chair, pushing herself in lazy circles as we all argued.

"What, I've got a job and shit. I haven't gotten around to it.

"Okay. Let's fucking do it, Brian said. He got off the bed and pushed through some junk under his desk and found the chemical kit. He pulled out a plastic test tube and scooped some coke off a pen cap into the tube. He made a big effort of rolling his eyes as he shook the tube, the liquid making a loud sloshing sound.

"If this comes back clean you owe me a key bump, he said.

"Uh-huh, I replied.

"Can we just listen to music? I don't even care, Tierra said.

Brian snickered as he peeled off the tape for the results.

"Fuck, Brian muttered. "I need to make a phone call tomorrow.

"Are you serious? I asked, feeling my voice rising. "Did you give her meth, you trailer-park dipshit?

"Jesus. I was kidding. It's clean, he replied tossing the vial

I checked and sure enough the little slot next to coke was red, the rest of them were plain.

"Look, everything's fine, we can move on, Erika said.

"Yeah, I agreed. "Sorry. Let's just relax.

"That's what we're trying to do. Why were you freaking out? You weren't even doing it.

"I don't know. Cause I care about what happens to you, I said.

"You just wanted a blow job, Erika said, producing a laugh from Brian and Tierra.

Before I had a chance to reply Naomi grabbed my arm and jerked her head toward the door. I grudgingly left with her while Erika mockingly waved me out. She sat down on the living room couch and I sat in a chair facing her. I waited for her to speak, but instead she pulled our bong closer to her and began packing a bowl.

"What? I finally asked.

"You're caring too much.

"Cause I don't want my friends doing meth?

She took a rip from the bong and tried blowing the smoke out through her nose. She was close to finished when she coughed the rest out.

"Damn, I'm getting better at that. You want one?

I nodded and she began packing another bowl. "Look, Tierra was bugging and—

"I know.

"Then why are you on my case?

"You're being a buzzkill, Danny. If you don't—

"For worrying about them.

"I guess. We're happy for you, Danny, we really are, but we don't need you telling us what we're doing to ourselves. I've got two years left, the idea of overdosing doesn't really bother me that much anymore.

"But Tierra—

"She's young and she's Tierra; she doesn't care right now. There's a chance she might grow out of it and there's a chance she doesn't, but pressing her is only gonna piss her off.

"So, what am I supposed to do? Just wait?

"Guide her in the right direction, or leave her be, she said sliding the bong over. "You're not gonna be her boyfriend if you don't understand her.

"I never said I wanted to be, I said taking my own hit.

Naomi just shrugged.

"So what are you telling me? I asked after.

"Keep getting better, but don't act like you're better than us.

"Naomi, I don't—

"It's okay; you are.

Naomi got up and hugged me.

"Get high, relax, then come back in if you're feeling better. With that she left the room.

* * *

When I was a kid I was afraid of heights. Not deathly afraid or crying or anything, just enough to feel butterflies and second guess things. There was this hill in our neighborhood that we would ride on our bikes and it ended in a sharp left. I was always worried I'd hit the steel barrier at the bottom and flip over my handlebars. My friends used to give me shit because I would always hold the brakes the whole way down. So I told them I'd ride down it without brakes.

This evolved and it left me betting seventeen bucks that I couldn't ride down the hill on my stomach on a skateboard. Luke convinced me I'd have better grip without a shirt and so I put my naked stomach on the board. I was so self-conscious about my belly that once I took my shirt off I refused to get off. I made them push me up to the edge. I had my shoes on both hands to act as breaks toward the end. I remember being giddy as I first sailed down, confident I was in control.

After I wiped out I looked up the hill watching my friends running down. My belly was covered in streaks from the skateboard grip and the asphalt. I felt numb, seemingly uncaring at what was happening to me. I pushed faintly at my gums where the missing tooth was. My dad was pissed because he was supposed to be meeting friends for happy hour when he was driving me to the hospital.

I wish I remembered all of that sooner.

* * *

I must've been sitting there for almost an hour, people coming in and out to grab drinks. It's a wonder I hadn't fallen asleep, drinking and bong rips usually put me under. I made my way back into the room. Ericka and Naomi cheered, Tierra blew a raspberry. I waved and settled into the wall, preparing myself. Naomi was hopping on her butt on the bed, Tierra was helping Ericka chop lines, and Brian was walking back and forth in the middle of some rant about Stephen King, as if he had ever read a single one of his books.

"Guys, I think I got to give myself another shot at getting clean, I can't do this anymore.

Naomi smiled, the other three gave blank stares.

"Pussy, Tierra laughed. "Don't start being lame, you got time to do that shit later.

Naomi mouthed, "It's okay, but didn't interrupt Tierra.

"I'm gonna break up with you, Tierra said.

Brian oohed like I just got called to the principal's office.

"We're not together.

"Well you wanna be. Right? Tierra replied. "I now pronounce us together and that if you become boring I'm breaking up with you.

"Okay, I'm going to bed.

I was teased by the four of them as I got up and closed the door behind me.

Chapter 20

"Your parents? I heard Naomi ask as she stared out the window at the U-Haul in the parking lot.

"Uh-huh.

The U-Haul was honestly an overreaction, I didn't have room nor purpose for half the shit in my room. My room at my parent's house already had mostly everything I needed. I just woke up with the distinct purpose of leaving which left little room for rational thought. I dropped the laundry into the back of the pickup and helped Naomi toss my bed sheets into the back with them.

"You didn't want those folded did you?

I shrugged and made my way back into my apartment. "Thanks for helping.

"Of course, just as long as you promise not to cut me off.

"What? I asked.

"Like in programs, they say cut out the shitty friends. My mom made me go to one, she said with a roll of her eyes.

"I'm not cutting you out, Naomi.

"Good, cause I'd kick you in the balls or something.

"Uh-huh, I said.

"Are you gonna go to a program? You're still under 25. Your parent's insurance probably covers it.

"I don't know, I figured I'd just shoulder through it.

"Going to rehab will make it easier though.

"I guess. Am I still allowed to smoke?

"Yeah, plus the one I went to allowed caffeine too.

"Alright, why not. Right? Not like I'm gonna be working

while I'm coming off everything.

We were walking back into the apartment at this point. Brian was in the living room wearing a T-shirt and boxers. The shirt was already stained with milk from his bowl of cereal.

"What're you doing?

"Moving out. I told you last night.

"What? I thought you were just being a pussy.

"Brian, don't be a dick, Naomi said.

"How am I being a dick?! He's the one moving out.

"I'm going to rehab, I decided out loud.

"Oh fuck. Are you serious? What you worried you'll die a year early or some dumb shit?

"Fuck off, man.

"No. Let's fucking talk about this.

Brian had put down the bowl and was approaching me aggressively. "You know what, everything else fits in my car. I'll just get it later.

I hugged Naomi and turned toward the exit. Brian started to yell something before I slammed the door. I pulled my hoodie in tighter as I made my way down the hallway. The door flew back open and I heard Brian come out the door followed behind by Naomi. I turned to see Naomi holding him back as Brian yelled at me. I pulled the earbuds out of my pocket and plugged them into my phone. I blasted some shitty punk rock in my ears as I tried to tune him out. It occurred to me that the posters I left in my room might be ripped to shreds when I came back, but I shrugged off the thought.

As I got in the U-Haul it made sense to me why Brian was so mad. Maybe because he felt like he couldn't get out. His parents were far past giving a shit and he would have a hard time switching careers, but the real reason was probably the promise I made him years ago. We were talking about all the fucking phonies who pretended to care about their white collar jobs and their mundane lives and I swore, I swore that we would never become that. Yet here I was leaving him high and dry.

Embarrassingly, I found myself getting lost on the way to my parent's. I plugged my old address into my phone and figured out I was going the right direction. I just had to go in the direction of Apple stores and Barnes and Noble and suddenly everything had that nostalgic shine to it. I pulled into my old house around noon. I saw my dad's car wasn't there and I was surprisingly disappointed. I got out of the truck and forced myself to the door. I rang several times, but no one was home. I ended up calling my sister.

"What?

"Do you know where Mom and Dad hide the keys to the front door?

"Why?

"Because I want to go in.

"This isn't one of those things where you steal the microwave and sell it to a pawnshop?

"Fuck off, I just wanted to surprise them ... I moved out of my apartment.

"Like willingly?

"Yeah, 'like willingly.' I wanna give rehab a chance, okay?

"Seriously?

"Yeah.

"Okay. I'm gonna come over now. Just wait for me.

"Okay.

I hung up the phone and took a look around before heading back into the U-Haul. I placed my earbuds in and played down across the seats, nursing my hangover and trying to sleep.

About fifteen minutes later Reagan pulled in. She knocked on the window waking me from my slumber as I sat up in the truck. I got out and she gave me a massive hug.

"This is gonna be really hard, but I'm with you the whole way. I'm so proud of you.

"Uh-huh. Can you help me move my shit?

"Yeah, sure, she said with an eyeroll. "Do you wanna move in everything or just go to rehab and let me and Mom and Dad move your stuff in?

"Let's just move it in right now. I still have to return the U-Haul.

So she unlocked the door with the key behind the grill and we slowly started moving everything into the house. Mostly everything was dumped into a pile in my room which felt about right. I had no real furniture of my own that I felt I needed so everything was mostly clothes with a few knick-knacks along for the ride. I saw Reagan look nostalgically at a little wooden parrot she had given me forever ago for Christmas, although neither of us mentioned it.

"Wanna follow me to the U-Haul shop and then we can go to rehab? I asked after we had moved the last of the junk.

She said sure and she followed me in her car on the way over. I exchanged the keys, probably got dinged for gas, and then we were in Reagan's car ready to go.

"So, where are we going?

"I've got a rehab that Naomi recommended once.

"Naomi's not sober though?

"Well, no, but she still said she really liked it.

"Okay then, my sister replied. "You know they expect you to actually open up in rehab.

"I know, I can open up.

"Since when?

"I open up to my friends all the time. Reagan was silent.

"I mean, I would open up to you, but I was scared of what I'd say, I said.

"Uh-huh, glad to know I'm second fiddle.

"It's not like that.

"What's it like then?

"I can't tell you that I feel like my life is pointless and that I feel like it's worthless to stop drinking?

"Do you feel that way?

"I used to, yeah, but I can't tell you that without scaring you.

"I've always been scared for you, Danny.

"Nope, just since I turned 18 and my numbers started showing.

"No, Danny, she said with a sigh. "I've been scared for you since I've been old enough to be scared for myself.

"Well, I guess that's family. Right?

"Sure.

The rest of the ride was silent. I was a little nauseous from the night before so I rolled down the window and let the summer breeze blow through the car. Reagan was playing light pop music over the stereo which I had pretended to hate. I was fucking scared. Rehab is similar to prison in that you can't leave and you're stuck in there with psychos. A lot of good people, a lot of people trying to improve themselves, but a lot of people who are close to that edge. I was worried I'd fail and then where would I be?

We pulled in.

"Can you walk in with me?

"Of course

And so we walked in together.

Chapter 21

They asked me a few questions before admitting me, mostly about self-harm. I was stripped to my boxers and checked for cuts; they gave me scrubs to wear. I was told I would get clothing privileges back after a day or so and then I was escorted to my room. My room had a drug test waiting for me which I took and gave back to the nurse.

My room had two beds, a desk, and a bathroom. I was told I may have a roommate later and then was shown around. It was mostly just hallways and bedrooms with a large front desk manned by multiple nurses. There was also a common room of sorts with tables filled with crafts and a TV with Netflix. For some reason I assumed that the TV would be set on kids mode, but the other patients were watching *Pulp Fiction*. For all intents and reasons, it was just a hospital, except for the lack of doorknobs and them giving us crayons instead of pens.

* * *

The most profound thing about the rehab was the boredom. I suppose life is boring and that's why people strive for adrenaline, drugs, and entertainment. On the second day, I got my clothes back and had an appointment with a psychologist. I tried to tell her everything I could and let her pick through what she determined was important and what wasn't. Luckily the only chemical I was still daily-abusing was alcohol, which led to some restless nights. Sleeping sober is a surprisingly difficult task—you just spend the night staring at the ceiling wondering what you did wrong.

I spent a lot of my time walking up and down the hallway, occasionally listening to the radio. Everything was regimented from outdoor time to group therapy. The only things that weren't regimented were music and books. Of the dozen books to pick from, most seemed uninteresting; nonetheless, I burned through three of them while I was inpatient. Music was better. They had headphones that could tune into the radio. I found an alternative rock station and would just zone out listening for hours at a time.

There were a few people with hard-core disabilities that I tended to stray away from, but most of the people in the rehab were shockingly normal. People who were just too depressed, too anxious, or simply trying to get clean like me. There were people with nine-to-fives, people with kids, everyone with faulty serotonin receptors or shit like that. I don't really know the science behind it.

We'd spend a lot of time talking. Mostly how we fucked up and landed ourselves in rehab. Some of the stigmas of ordinary life had been taken off, though, which led to some surprisingly honest conversations. We'd compare numbers (a lot of shorters, no surprise there), compare our favorite drugs, and talk about mental health difficulties which we all obviously had big time.

Every day you think maybe tomorrow will be different.

* * *

"There are two wolves inside of you— the group counselor named Omar started.

I rolled my eyes and whispered to the man sitting next to me.

"—the one you feed— Omar continued.

My neighbor nodded and whispered back, "I've heard it before too.

"Excuse me, Danny, the Omar said. "Do you have something you'd like to share with everyone else?

Omar supposedly had done some time for a DUI. He never got his numbers because he showed up to the DDD drunk on his eighteenth birthday. They said he couldn't consent. So even though he's not Gnostic, no numbers. He said he's done every drug under the sun, but after he struck a ten-year-old biking one night, he's never touched anything else again. The kid lost mobility of his legs, but somehow survived. Omar got a job at the rehab center once he got out to help him stay clean. Now he led junkies like me in group therapy.

"Sorry, I've just heard this story before, I said. "I heard it in the psych ward.

"Has anyone else heard it? Omar asked.

A few people nodded.

"If you've heard the story please raise your hand, Omar said.

There were seven of us in there and five of us raised our hands. Omar laughed.

"Well, Danny, it seems that you're correct, this story may be more popular than I realized.

"Sorry for bursting your bubble, I said.

"No apology necessary, although I have to ask, what do you think the parable means? Omar asked.

"I mean, it's essentially arguing the existence of karma. You reap what you sow kinda thing. If we treat our body poorly and abuse drugs, the evil wolf will win and, overall, we'll be a shitty person.

"You're moving in the right direction, but I've met tee-totalers who are absolute assholes and I've met drug addicts with hearts of gold. It's more advanced than simply choosing to abstain from drugs. You need to seek out the beauty in this world and respond in kind. You need to change your perspective.

I nodded.

"So what do you all want to talk about? Omar asked.

The man next to me (I need to get better at learning names) chimed in.

"How about we talk about the Unvarnished Truth bill. It's supposed to go in front of the supreme court this week.

"What do you think of it? Omar asked.

"It's conservative bullshit, the man replied. "They get to ignore other rules, but enforce their own beliefs in the jury.

"What is that bill? a girl named Jody asked.

"For born-again Gnostics, they swear to never reveal their numbers and to pretend they don't exist, Omar began. "However, Waterson religious people believe that those numbers have a direct correlation to your morality, so they want to peek at the numbers even though they are forbidden too by Gnostic scripture. The bill essentially allows for judges to peek at the born-again Gnostic's numbers and tell them to the jury, which not only will be violating the Gnostic's religious beliefs, but will likely directly impact the outcome of the trial.

"So, basically it's racist? I questioned. "Everyone knows the lower your numbers the chances of you being found guilty exponentially rises. It's a bullshit system and we shouldn't comply.

"Well what's your solution? Omar asked.

"We hide the numbers of everyone on trial so that no religious propaganda can determine the outcome of the trial.

"Even though most people are religious?

"Precisely for that reason, I responded.

"Have you ever heard the phrase 'Work within the system' before? Omar asked. "The point being that while there are thousands of different ways the world works and even if something might be right or wrong, you still have to work within those rules. We produce enough food to feed the entire world with food left over, so you could conceivably tax the billionaires and force them to pay for everyone to eat. It would probably make the world a better place, but the billionaires control the politics and every American naïvely believes that they will be rich someday. So any attempt to get the rich to pay their 'fair share' will be laughed out of Congress. To feed the poor you must work within the rules or change the rules, but changing the rules takes generations and a revolution, and then you better be lucky that those don't backfire and become the very thing you fought against.

"Like that old song by The Who? I asked.

"Exactly.

"So, what's the takeaway: the world's fucked? I asked.

"A wise priest once said, 'When I feed the poor they call me a hero, but when I ask why the poor are hungry they call me a communist.' The takeaway is to try to find ways to better the world without breaking the system and to trust God has a plan. That's what I do, I spend my time helping junkies, like I once was, and praying that God does not lead his flock astray.

"I don't believe in God.

"Then you must live a very lonely life.

"Doesn't make him real.

"Same as not believing in him doesn't make him false.

I nodded.

"Well, boozers and users, time is up. I'll catch you back again tomorrow.

"Not me, A girl piped up.

"That's right Nora, congratulations. I'll be roct—

I put on my headphones and walked out of the room. The Beastie Boys blasted in my ears as I began the walk to my room. I had felt clean now, no more urges, no more shakes, no more angry outbursts. I wanted to go, but they wanted to hold me a little longer. So I stayed here in purgatory waiting for my time to run up. It was supposed to be another nine days and then I would be moved into a halfway home for a bit, just until I got my balance back. That didn't bother me, I probably needed it.

I had gotten all of those addictive chemicals out of my brain, but those urges to snort blow and drink tequila straight from the bottle were still deeply implanted inside my little lizard brain. They had tried to teach us coping methods like exercising or calling a friend, but my friends all wanted to do drugs and if I ran every time I felt an urge I'd be running marathons daily. As I was going over these problems I saw Omar waving at me. I took off my headphones and approached him.

"What's up, boss? I asked.

"When do you get out?

"Next Thursday, it'll be a full month.

"You think that's long enough?

"I don't know. I said. "Do you?

"It doesn't matter what I think, it just matters what you feel, he responded. "Do you feel ready?

"No, and I doubt I will next Thursday.

"Well, that's good. Those cocky bastards who strut out of

here thinking that things are just gonna be easy always end up back here on their asses, Omar said.

"So how do I do it?

"Trust yourself and stay vigilant. Keep going to meetings and make sure your life stays active. When you need help, ask for it and you'll be okay.

I nodded and Omar walked off. I put my headphones on and started listening to some Green Day. I walked back to my room and moved the desk. Behind it I wrote:

Joypunks like us will always find our way here.
May we also someday find our way home.

With that I laid down on my bed and let the music play me to sleep.

* * *

Nine days later I sat at the edge of my bed. The music was blasting from my headphones. I was vaguely aware that music was playing, but I was more focused on my future. For the first time in a long while it didn't seem so bleak. A nurse walked in and said that my sister was here. I took off the headphones and placed them on the desk. I picked up a couple of papers with poetry I had written and exited the room.

My sister was in the hallway. She beamed at me and brought me into a big hug. I noticed Naomi hanging around behind my sister.

"She invited you? I asked.

"I promised to be a good influence and she said I could tag along.

I hugged Naomi and I approached the nurse's station. They

gave me my daily antidepressants and a baggie with some more, along with nicotine patches. I thanked them, and Reagan signed me out. Omar shook my hand and then we left. The air was crisp and I pulled in Naomi tight for warmth. She reciprocated and handed me her vape. I took a deep lungful until I felt it burn before I exhaled in a ragged cough. Reagan gave me a disapproving look.

"Reagan, I was in there for liquor, cocaine, and psychedelics. Nicotine is fine and I won't live long enough for the bad effects anyways.

Naomi laughed and took an inhale of her own while Reagan rolled her eyes. We piled into Reagan's car. I sat in the back seat while Naomi sat up front. The halfway house was only ten minutes away, so it was going to be a short drive.

"Can we stop at the Circle K for a pack of cigs? I asked.

"As long as you're sober, we can pick up whatever you want, Reagan replied.

Naomi turned around and winked at me. I settled into the backseat and I felt something I hadn't felt in a while. I think it was hope.

Chapter 22

A couple of months later

I was sitting in a bowling alley with a nonalcoholic beer in my hand. Luke was up and was choosing a random ball. About a month after I got out of rehab I had reached out to him and we'd started meeting every Tuesday night. A couple times his girlfriend came and Naomi and Charlie always had an open invitation. I suspected Luke hadn't told his girlfriend that Naomi and he used to be a thing, but maybe he was a better man than me. Naomi usually came, although she was currently flaking. Last time though she got us in trouble for lighting up a joint in the bathroom, so maybe she just needed a week off. It was just Luke, Charlie, and me. Charlie was wearing jeans and a flannel with no wig. Luke was wearing khakis and a windbreaker.

"Your turn, boss, Luke said as he approached the seats again.

"I swear we could go bowling every week for a year and I'd still be shit at this game, I replied.

"Aww. Does somebody need bumpers? Charlie asked.

"I need bumpers for life, man.

They laughed as I picked up a glitter-splattered orange ball. I tossed it down the lane for a solid four and followed it up with a two.

"See, I'm dog shit at this game.

"You got to pick the movies last week. It was my turn and I wanted to go bowling, Charlie said.

"She's right, added Luke.

"Plus I only got a couple of months before I move to New York so you better cherish me while I'm here.

"Uh-huh, I said.

"Your parents still doing random drug tests? Luke asked.

"Yup, it's a little patronizing to be honest.

"Oh, boohoo, they're supporting you. Who cares if you have to piss in a bottle? Charlie said.

"I fucking care. They're treating me like I'm fragile.

"They're treating you like an addict and they earned that right, Charlie said.

"Just keep making strides and maybe they'll lay off soon.

"Yeah, one can hope, I replied. "They're still trying to get me to go to church.

"What else are you doing Saturday night? asked Charlie.

"No, but I'd be lying, I said. "I don't believe in any of that.

"I don't know if that qualifies as a lie, Luke said. "They just think that'd be positive for you. Indulge them.

"Well enough about me, how you two doing? I asked.

"Just signed a lease in Mott Haven in the south Bronx, it's a little studio, but it'll be cozy, Charlie said.

"I just bought a ring, Luke said.

"Kinda douchey, I responded, "but I see it for you.

"Oh my God, it's not for him, Charlie said. "He's fucking proposing, you idiot.

"Wait, what? You're proposing to your girlfriend? I asked.

"Yeah, he said with a twinkle in his eye. "I'm gonna shoot my shot, man.

"Congratulations, I said as I brought him in for a hug. "Can we see it?

"Bro, I didn't bring it bowling.

* * *

I texted Naomi as I was driving home telling her that I missed her and that bowling sucks.

I was blasting music as I drove cause permanent ear damage wasn't a great fear of mine and I figured I might as well slip in vices where I could. I was surprised when instead of texting me she called me back.

"Hey, Naomi, what's up?

"Brian isn't gonna be home for a while. Wanna come over and chill for a minute?

"Yeah, sure. Does he still hate me?

"I don't think he's spending much time thinking about you.

"Enough time has passed?

"No, he's just doing a ton of coke right now. I'm kinda of thinking of holding a light intervention.

"Yeah, that'll go great.

"Look, just swing by, alright?

About twenty minutes later I pulled into my old apartment building. I noticed some stranger had parked in my old reserved spot as I made my way over. I knocked rhythmically at the door and heard a clatter as Naomi came to the door.

"Sorry, I was just putting my bong down. How are you?

"Good. Got work in the morning so I'll only stay for a bit, but I'm genuinely good.

"Glad to hear it. Want something to drink?

Naomi got me a diet soda from the fridge as I looked around. Nothing much had changed since I had moved out.

"My room still empty?

"Yeah, we were gonna turn into a lounge of sorts. Brian put a broken pinball machine that he was gonna fix in there, but it's pretty much empty. Wanna play Xbox?

We sat down on the couch and opened up a simple shooter and went to work. Naomi was unabashedly kicking my ass while quite apologetically taking bong rips the whole time. In treatment I had thought of going California sober and smoking a little flower from time to time, but had eventually decided against it. Of all the substances I quit, pot was the least appealing to me, there are just so many better drugs out there.

"Brian still mad at me? I asked.

"I don't know, he's kind of a paranoid mess all the time. He even went as far to suggest we blackmail people to make sure they don't rat him out for slinging.

"Jesus, how much coke is he doing?

"I don't know, maybe with any luck he'll hit a breaking point and go to rehab.

"He's more likely to go into psychosis.

"It's not funny, Danny.

"I'm not laughing.

There was a moment of silence broken by animated sounds before I spoke again. "Enough about Brian though. How are you doing, Naomi?

"Oh, fine. Work is okay and I'm still just passing the time, but my friends with benefits just broke up with me.

"I didn't know you were seeing anyone.

Naomi gave a noncommittal shrug.

"He was an alcoholic anyways.

"Aren't we all? I replied and she laughed.

"Speaking of alcoholics, would you be willing to show up to Brian's intervention?

"Seriously? I thought he hated the idea of me.

"Well, psychologists say it's important to show a supportive front and I couldn't get his parents—

"You couldn't get his parents?

"They said they had already tried before.

"What makes you think you're gonna change his mind then?

"Cause I'm gonna move out if he says no and I have to try. He's got some years left and he's not gonna make it at this momentum.

I nodded, but didn't say anything.

Chapter 23

I sat in my old living room as my leg bounced and my head throbbed. I desperately wanted a drink, wouldn't that be a move. Relapsing at an intervention. Naomi had invited me over the very second that Brian had left. I reluctantly came.

Naomi was a ball of energy. She wanted a serious conversation and she felt that starting off the intervention with us playing video games or watching TV would set the wrong tone. So we just waited with no distractions. Naomi took this time to finally getting around to cleaning the apartment. She had dusted everything, cleaned stains, vacuumed, washed bongs, and ordered everything in the room in a way that was surely a declarable neurosis. She had asked me three times if a ponytail was too casual for this type of situation and I had to assure her that no straight male could possibly give a shit. Unless Brian was secretly bi, which I doubted, it could not make less of a difference. Naomi declared that homophobic and refused to elaborate.

Brian usually didn't take too long on deliveries, but he also didn't usually sample the product with the customers. Naomi said that may not be the case anymore, apparently the little fiend had recently developed quite the habit. Not that any of us were strangers to coke addiction, but there are levels. Luckily if you're a dealer you never hit the "sexual favors level because you always have a steady supply. Unluckily, most people reconsider their life choices when a blowjob is on the table, so a slow descent into that hell may have done him a favor.

I had been over for four hours at this point and had drank approximately a million diet cokes, smoked half a pack out on the balcony (sobriety sucks), and there was still little evidence of him showing. Naomi had chosen a day I had off from work so I had no excuse to leave. On a quick side note my job had given me time off for rehab so I was still actively employed. I still lived with my parents though, so despite the job I felt like a bum.

Naomi had tried texting him and calling him, but no dice. She probably would've sent him a fucking email if he had one. God knows how he got through the twenty-first century without one.

I vaguely remembered that Brian had used one of my old books to prop up his bed so I went into his room and pulled it out from under the IKEA frame. It was about a spaceship headed to Mars where everyone spoke a different language. The dialogue was good, but quite frankly the author was a hack. Still it was more enjoyable than making more small talk with Naomi who couldn't quite seem to get her mind right. She's usually more level-headed, more sure of herself. I think she sees this as a life or death situation, which it might be, and that if she doesn't find a way to make it work that Brian's soul's fucked, which it isn't. I'm sure there is a junkie heaven with no hangovers and hot cocktail waitresses.

There's a knock at the door. Naomi looks at me and I toss my book onto the table and shrug.

Naomi yells, "It's open and Brian barges in. He's clearly high.

He yells out, "Here's Johnny and strolls to the freezer and pulls out a bottle of Jack. He spins off the lid and flicks it at me and takes a big pull. I half expected him to choke on it, but he swallows like a pornstar and plops down on a lawn chair in front of Naomi and me.

"Brian, are you high? I ask without needing an answer.

"Like a kite, brother, he replies. "How you been? Haven't seen your candyass since you bitched out and decided to become a citizen.

"I've been good, I lied. "Sobriety's not that bad, I lied again

"Uh-huh, and Naomi how have you been?

"Since this morning?

"Uh-huh.

"Fine.

"Well, that's dandy, Brian replied. "I'd even go as far as to say it's peachy.

"Look, Brian, we were gonna talk to you, but maybe you should take a quick nap and we can— I started.

"No way in hell, man. I'm not gonna sleep through my own intervention.

I glanced at Naomi.

"Who told you? she asked.

"I thought there would be more people here. Where are my parents?

"They've given up.

"Crying shame. My brothers?

"I called Craig, but I didn't have the other two's numbers.

"Should've asked, Brian replied. He stared at us with a grin before taking another swig of the Jack.

"Who told you? Naomi asked again.

"You asked Tierra, you silly goose. She knows there are only a few sober drug dealers. You really think she wouldn't tip me off.

"You invited Tierra? I asked.

"I thought she cared, replied Naomi.

"You know she's moved on, Brian said. "She's found a new boy-toy, Danny. Apparently you're easily replaceable, but, me, I'm fucking indispensable.

"That's great; good for her.

"I bet her new boyfriend has a massive dick.

Naomi made a face.

"Okay. Do you hear yourself? I asked. "You sound like a fucking sociopath.

"Oh, do I? Do I? If you really cared about me you wouldn't be trying to get me off drugs, you'd be snorting fat lines with me.

"Dude, I don't even care if you do drugs. Do some drugs; I don't give a fuck. But when paramedics are issuing you Narcan I'm not gonna be holding your hand.

"Oh, you know all about that don't you, Danny? Miss-little-bitch-who-couldn't-handle-their-shit.

"He's lucky to be alive. Naomi said. "If we weren't there he'd be dead.

"And if you're doing drugs while you're alone in your room, you're headed toward the same, I said.

"Oh. I need a grown-up in the room when I'm doing booger sugar?

"No, just someone capable, and willing, to call 911, I said.

He snorted and then took out a dime bag. It plopped on the table and he started pulling out his wallet. I noticed the baggie's contents looked like instant hot chocolate.

"Oh, no, please go on, he said.

"Brian? I asked. "Is that heroin?

"Yeah, want a snowball?

"God-fucking-dammit, I heard Naomi mutter.

"Are you out of your fucking mind? I asked. "What happened to 'I'm waiting til I've got a week left on my clock?'

"Hey, people change. Look at you, you got off drugs.

"People change? I said.

"Sure. Tierra does heroin with me, ya know.

"God-fucking-dammit. Are you insane?! Naomi yelled.

"Maybe, Brian replied.

While Brian was talking with us he had dispensed a little heroin rock onto the table. After placing a dollar bill over it he ran a credit card over the president's face, flattening the surface. He then pulled the dollar away like the world's shadiest magician and began rolling up the dollar bill.

"Brian, please don't, I pleaded.

Brian put the dollar to his nose. He theatrically placed a finger to his other nostril and deeply inhaled. An instant grin appeared on his face and he sunk back into his chair. Naomi started crying.

"Look at what you're doing, I said while pointing at Naomi. Brian giggled. He fucking giggled.

I snagged the baggie and headed toward my old bathroom. I heard Brian laughing as I made my way through my old room. It was sparse like a tomb. I threw the baggie into the toilet and kicked the handle with my foot. I didn't even bother watching it flush as I made my way back into the living room. I sat back down and looked at Brian. He raised an eyebrow and snorted at his own joke.

"I've got more, he whispered.

I got up.

"It's in the safe and I changed the combo.

I sat back down.

Brian giggled again. I put my face in my hands and Naomi reached for one of the bongs, still crying. She pulled a nug out of the jar and placed it in a grinder.

"Can I have a hit? Brian asked.

"No, Naomi said.

She pinched out some green and dropped it into the bowl before sparking up. She blew the smoke up into the air before picking up the bong by its neck and swinging the bong at Brian's face. It connected with his temple. I expected it to break, but it remained intact as Brian sailed from his chair. I was already out of my chair before Brian hit the ground. I gently pulled the bong out of Naomi's grip before tossing it to the other side of the room. Loose water spilled onto the carpet. I grabbed the second bong and threw it toward it's brother. I looked at Naomi and heard them clink behind me.

"I'm pretty sure interventions are supposed to be a 'safe' environment, I said.

"Brian, are you okay?

"No. The fucking cunt belted me.

"You promised to never call me that.

"And you promised to never assault me with a bong, Brian said with blood pouring down his face.

"And you promised to never do heroin. You broke two promises and I broke one. You still owe me one.

"I also promised to never make a pact, but guess what? I did, Brian replied.

I stood still and then I started crying.

I heard Naomi quietly whisper, "What?

"We got robbed. I needed money.

I started sobbing.

Brian got up and stumbled to his room. I wanted to fucking kill him. I embraced Naomi and we cried together. It felt like an eternity, but I would happily spend eternity with her.

She was crying too, I felt the tears on my neck. Then Brian came back with a gun. I pushed Naomi behind me, but before I could say anything he put the gun to his bleeding temple.

"I deserve to die, he said.

Chapter 24

Have I mentioned that Gnostics go to church at 11:30 at night? Every Saturday at 11:30 pm the church parking lots fill up and everyone enters the holy building. The idea being that once your date hits, you die instantly. So if your date is August 20th, on August 20th at midnight, you'll drop dead. It also corresponds to whatever time zone you were born in. If you were born in L.A. and you live in Manhattan, then you'll die at exactly three in the morning East Coast Time.

There have been a lot of studies as to what exactly happens at midnight, but essentially your body's internal clock is perfectly in sync with the date on your wrist. The second it becomes the date all your organs simply shut down. Even Gnostics who don't know their date, their date is still encoded into their DNA. So when a Gnostic dies, the numbers suddenly appear on their wrist glowing blue. Most Gnostics actually pull over if they're driving at 11:59 p.m. They won't get back on the road 'til 12:01 p.m. Gnostics also can't legally donate organs because the organs will shut down once they hit that date. For some organs, like kidneys, the donor would have time to get to the hospital, but if the lungs or heart shut down at exactly midnight you're gonna be in real trouble.

Anyway, the point being is that Gnostics always have their sermons at midnight so that if someone dies, at least they'll be surrounded by their community. Sometimes kids die before they even get a chance to see their numbers, but that's rare.

Of course, this means that the Gnostics who don't die on a Sunday usually die in their sleep. Their significant others just wake up to find numbers on their wrist and their heart no longer beating. That's not such a bad way to go. Most Waterson and nonreligious people die surrounded by their loved ones. This isn't always good though. Some people aren't ready. They scream and they cry and they beg whatever gods are listening to stop the clock, change their date, or perform some sorta miracle. There never are any miracles. People just stop screaming and abruptly fall to the ground. Their time had come. You can't bribe death.

Of course, there are exceptions, people who bravely defy death's terror and their last words to their loved ones are poignant and beautiful. They say that a death well-handled is a sign of a life well lived. That's how I want to go. I've had enough of chaos in my life and I just hope in the end I find peace. I suppose that all depends on what happens after life, I don't know if I believe in an after.

I say all of this to preface the pure awe I hold for one man. I don't remember his name, but I remember watching him die. He was a born-again Gnostic, just like Patrick. So when he was eighteen he went to the DDD and signed up to get his numbers. He put his hand in the machine and it spit out the exact day that he would die. They said he would die when he was thirty on a cool night in April. He presumably made bad decisions as a result of this information and, in the end, he decided to leave that life behind. He strapped leather on his wrist, said he was a born-again Gnostic, and then refused to discuss his numbers with anyone. He pretended he didn't know them anymore. But of course he knew them. How could anyone forget their death date?

On the day he was going to die, he got up and went to church. I don't know what the rest of his day was like, presumably those friends who knew his day reached out to him on the day or possibly weeks before. I don't know how he reacted. Did he admit he was on death's doorstep or did he pretend that he still didn't know? Whatever his reaction was, in his final moments, he hopped in his car and drove to church. He sung holy hymns, he shook the hands of those close to him, wished them grace, then dropped like an empty sack.

The Gnostics have a moment of silence from 11:59 to 12:01 every service. They all bow their heads and pray. If you go to enough services you know that eventually someone will die. That's statistics. But usually the member who dies has no knowledge of their impending doom. Born-again Gnostics know. I don't know how he didn't scream out in fear. He just stood there and took it. Accepted his fate and didn't thrash at it.

He was standing behind me. I was fifteen. His chin struck the back of my head as he fell.

Hard, but not hard enough to draw blood. I initially was pissed, until I realized what had happened. Then we saw the leather bound around his wrist and in that moment I realized it wasn't chance. He was alone except for his wife—she had been crying throughout the service. I had chalked it up to a hard day because she was quiet, but after he fell I knew. We all knew; she must've known.

Because he had a leather-bound wrist, they had to treat it as a medical emergency, no one could see his wrist to know if his numbers were blue. Doctors were called and they looked for a pulse. People asked his wife if it was his day. She said that she was forbidden by Gnostic scripture to reveal his day, but she said it through heavy sobs. Eventually the head priest broke the key off his necklace. He slowly released the lock bound on his wrist. He checked the date and locked it back up before placing the key in a pocket in his robes. He said that the man had not fainted, that his date had come and he had passed.

We held a ten-minute moment of silence for the man while men from the choir were called forth. Six predetermined men from the choir came up and lifted him on their shoulders. They carried him to the altar and placed him down gently before returning to their place in the grandstands. The room was silent except for his wife who was sobbing hysterically. Those who were close comforted her, but no one else looked her way.

It's worth noting that she was a born-again Gnostic too. On her wrist was the same leather and around her neck she wore a key. I presumed that they had met before their conversion and had found religion together. She had probably known for a long time that he was destined to go first, but she had probably ignored it. Confronting reality can be difficult. Patrick had newly joined the church at that time and I remember he went back to comfort her. I remember even then I had held him in high regard; I still do.

I don't quite remember the sermon that followed, I was too focused on the man behind me. I think the sermon was about courage, I don't care. I just hope I can be that brave someday. I know my day is creeping up on me. I can only avoid it for so long. I'm done numbing myself. Time to face the world.

Chapter 25

"Brian don't—

He smirked and pulled the trigger. The gun clicked. Brian pulled it down from his temple and stared at it. "I don't keep it loaded.

Before he turned around I was across the room and tackled him, slamming us both into the TV stand. The glass cracked and we both rolled to the ground. Naomi was screaming. Brian flipped around and pistol whipped me in the face. My nose spurted blood onto the carpet.

"Naomi, call the police! I yelled.

Now, in a fair fight, Brian would kick my ass. I'm pretty scrawny (put on some weight though when I got off coke) and Brian is about six inches taller than me. On the other hand, Brian just took a fat line of heroin and that has to weaken your fighting resolve considerably. I also believed that Brian truly didn't want to die and that he would eventually give in. Regardless, I punched his face and felt his nose crumple underneath my fist. I had never punched someone before and recoiled at the pain it caused my wrist. Blood was dripping off my face and mixing into his, which pooled into the carpet. Bet Naomi felt pretty silly for vacuuming earlier. I sniggered at my joke and punched him again and again.

I could hear Naomi in the background as I wrestled with Brian. I was trying to flip him and put him in a headlock which was considerably harder than it should've been. I would randomly give up and resort back to punching him in the face. He was trying to punch back, but I had so much weight on him

that it was difficult for him to get a clean shot. He was moaning now which was surely a good sign for me. I just needed to
hold him in place until the po-po arrived.

He dropped the gun and I immediately pounced on it,
throwing it across the room. Finally I was able to flip him over.
I wrapped my arm around his neck. I rolled onto my back so
that he was on top of me and held him in place in a headlock.
Brian stopped fighting and started moaning again. Naomi was
in hysterics in the background.

"I'm sorry, man, Brian said.

"I know, man. I'm sorry too. Are you okay?

"No, but it's okay. I love you, man, I love you, both.

"I love you, too, I replied.

"Can you let me up?

"When the cops get here I will.

"That's okay. I really fucked up, man.

"I know. It's okay.

He started crying and I felt his body shake as I held him to
me. I squeezed tighter and refused to give him an inch, worried he'd get a second wind and try for the gun again. In the
background, Naomi cried into the telephone to some operator
who was seemingly telling her to take deep breaths and calm
down. I felt meditative, my muscles were taught and my mind
was floating free. I wondered what was going to happen to us.
The cops would almost certainly search the apartment, especially considering Brian's gun is almost certainly unregistered.
Would Naomi and I be dragged away to some godforsaken
prison for staying with Brian 'til the cops came? Spending our
days apart because of the sin of trying to save a sinner? Fly
with the crows, right? Brian seemed uniquely fucked, however. I think he knew better than to talk to cops, but he wasn't

exactly in a stable state. This all felt so inevitable and paradox-ically avoidable. If I knew this was potentially my last day free, I, too, might've taken up Brian on his offer for some heroin.

Then the cops came in, they quietly pulled Naomi aside while motioning toward Brian and I with tasers. I relinquished my grip and stood up, putting my hands to my head. They were sticky and wet. Brian curled up in a fetal position. A cop motioned for me to turn around. I looked at the snow peaked mountains as I felt the metal click on my wrist. Another cop reached down and picked up Brian's gun with a glove. He inspected it and made sure it was empty before placing it back on the ground.

The paramedics came in and asked if I was the suicidal one and I tilted my head toward Brian who was still on the ground. They came down next to him and started talking in low voices that I couldn't hear. A cop came up and talked over them, ask-ing me if I was hurt, on drugs, why I was there, etc. I began responding before silently cursing myself and then began yell-ing at Naomi not to respond to any of the cops question. They hurried me out as I told her that cops are allowed to lie and that she couldn't answer anything, no matter how small, without a lawyer present. A female cop led me outside and slammed my ass down on the concrete. She stood over me like a colossus as I tried to take deep breaths and calm myself down. I caught myself beginning to pray before I started laughing, no one was listening.

Another cop came out and read me my Miranda rights before taking me by the shoulder and leading me outside the apartment complex. My old neighbors were watching and I became self-conscious about the blood on me. I was grateful only Brian's name was on the lease as the cop put his hand on my blood stained hair and pushed me into the back of the ccp car. They wouldn't roll down the windows and I threw up on the upholstery in the backseat on the way to the station.

Chapter 26

I sat in a cheap metal chair with my hands handcuffed to the desk in front of me. I had given up on asking them to let me go, they hadn't given up on asking me questions and lies.

"Naomi said you supplied the drugs?

"Why were you at Brian's apartment?

"Did you know that Brian was on drugs?

"If we were to drug test you would we find anything?

Did someone make a 'pact'?

My answer to every question was the same: give me my phone call, I need to call my lawyer.

They kept saying the phone was busy and that they'd tell me when it was free. In the meantime, they had a million questions and a million lies. I don't think cops are bad people, in fact they clearly saved Brian's life, but right now their only goal was to absolutely destroy my life. I had too much left to do to waste it on this bullshit. I just hoped Naomi had stuck to my advice, she had just as much to lose.

Eventually, three hours in, the cops got me up and led me to the phonebank. They told me I had five minutes which was plenty of time. Still in handcuffs, I pulled a business card out of my wallet that I had kept on me since my first DUI. My lawyer's name was Molly and I don't know if she was great, but she had seemingly done a competent job my first time around.

The phone rang and a secretary picked up.

"Hello? he asked.

"Hi, my name is Danny. I've just been arrested and need to speak to Molly Rodriguez immediately.

He patched me through to Molly.

"Hello, you've just been arrested?

"Yeah, this is Danny. You helped me with a DUI a couple years back. I was the one who was flirting with a girl arrested on arson charges in the courtroom.

"I remember you. What's the situation?

"A friend and I went to another friend's apartment for an intervention. He started doing a bunch of drugs and then tried to kill himself. We called the cops. They arrested all three of us. There was a bunch of drugs in there and I'm guessing an unregistered gun or two. We need immediate services.

"The Flagstaff City Jail?

"Yes.

"I can be there in twenty.

"That's perfect. Thank you.

She hung up immediately. I clicked the receiver with my thumb and began dialing my mom's phone number. The cop watching me took the phone from my hand and hung it up.

"We said one phone call.

"You said five minutes.

"And one phone call.

I grumbled and reluctantly followed him back to the inter-view room. The cop instead led me past that into a cell with several fellow degenerates and opened the door. Honestly, I was relieved to not talk to my mom.

"Given up on questioning me? I asked.

"We're gonna throw the book at you, asshole. Don't be so cocky.

"All I did was stop a suicide.

The cop slammed the door and I took a seat on the bench. The inmate next to me was a scrawny Native American kid in a wife beater who was sucking the life out of a cigarette. I asked him for a spare and he obliged, pulling out a Marlboro box with a lighter in it. I happily thanked him and lit him up. We started with some small talk, he was there for being arrested at a peaceful protest for trespassing, but apparently he had some unpaid parking tickets and an active warrant so they were giving him the full treatment. His name was Paul and he agreed that my situation was equally bullshit. We mostly talked about movies and cheap beer which turned into a conversation on sobriety and existentialism. He was actually a cool hang, I got his number to participate in future protests with him.

Molly showed up in a suit and was shadowed by a cop.

Before she could talk I said, "Go find Naomi. I'll be fine. Help Naomi.

She nodded and scurried off with the cop.

"You're a good friend, Paul said.

"If you knew her you'd understand, I replied.

* * *

An hour later Molly reappeared. The cops took us to a private room. Molly had them finally take the handcuffs off and I sat down across a table from her. There was one of those one way mirrors in the back of the room, but she assured me they weren't allowed to listen in or gather evidence.

"How are Naomi and Brian? I asked.

"Naomi's fine. She talked and cried a lot, but she didn't implicate herself. She wanted me to thank you for your advice and for getting her legal representation. A lot of both your and her case will heavily rely on the fact that you were trying to prevent an active suicide attempt. It will play well with a jury and it also gives you a fair amount of immunity. Naomi unfortunately lives there, so her case will be harder. However, since you recently moved out you've got a little more wiggle room. Will you be able to pass a drug test?

"Yeah, I'm a couple months sober.

"Good for you. I know that's no easy task, especially with your circumstances. My brother was a shorter as well so—

"What about Brian?

"Brian's in real trouble. There's some ethical violations with interrogating someone after an attempted suicide attempt, but nonetheless he signed a full confession. They're gonna send him to the psychiatric facility soon, but once he leaves he's gonna spend the rest of his life in prison. I'm sorry.

"I'm not. You know he signed a pact?

"I do, but he seems to possess an honest soul. Desperate people do desperate things. I hope you can still seem him as human and a friend.

I nodded.

"I can get you and Naomi in front of a judge in two day's time. I suspect your story, especially with your recent sobriety, will grant us leniency and you'll be able to make bail.

I nodded again.

"Is there anything else I can do for you?

"Can you call my Mom and try to explain this mess to her?

"I can try.

"Thanks.

"Stay strong, Danny. It's my job to fix messes like this. Just remember you did nothing wrong.

I nodded again and we left the room. The cops led me back to my cell and I smoked another cigarette with Paul as I tried to fall asleep in the corner.

Epilogue

A couple more years later

I pulled my same POS car into the parking lot, the car would probably outlast me at this point. I let the keys hang in the ignition as the last few bars played over the stereo. Finally I twisted the keys and released them, sliding them into my pocket. I grabbed a cigarette from my pack, only one left pointing up. The superstition made me smile as I dipped out of the car. I lit the cigarette as I left my car and headed toward the ugly government building.

I dropped it outside the entrance and twisted my boot to put out the embers still flicking from the filter. I picked it up off the ground, wet from the slush on the ground, and dropped it into the empty cigarette box, I figured littering outside a prison was probably asking for trouble anyways. One of the guards went out of his way to tell me no smoking inside as if that wasn't a no brainer, but I just nodded and thanked him.

As I made my way down the penitentiary hallway I was surprised by the amount of normal looking people following along in our group. I suppose I expected thugs and addicts to be visiting their buddies on the inside, but we resembled a collection of strangers dragged out of a supermarket. Only difference, no one was busy and everyone looked tired.

We went through some security checkpoints with metal detectors and dogs, whole nine yards. They happily disposed of my cigarette pack for me and double-checked everything as if my keys were hiding a secret knife or something. In the end, everyone was cleared and we made our way deeper into the building.

* * *

"Long time no see.

"You got a prison wife yet?

"Fuck off, man, Brian replied. "You know you'll be the only one for me.

I gave a slight smirk.

"So how you been, man? I asked.

"Good, man. Just biding my time.

"'Til?

"Apparently, if I show 'good behavior' I could get out three days before my date. Police custody of course, but I could still say good-bye to a couple people and have a beer or two.

"That's nice, man. Gives you something to work toward.

"I suppose. Although a lot of people get denied parole at the last minute. Sucks we've had our last drink together.

"Nah, man. I'm gonna Houdini this shit. I said pointing to my wrist. "First round's on me.

"Alright bet ... so today, huh?

"Hey, I wrote. I shouldn't have.

"I know, just giving you grief. Still didn't think you'd wait this long, he admitted. "Do you ever think it's funny how people only forget birthdays. Not the death dates.

"Well, birthdays don't really matter.

Brian nodded at this.

"I got some stuff I need to ap—

"I read the letters, you're good.

"Yeah, but I wanna—

"Brian. I said cutting him off again. "You're good. We're good.

He nodded halfheartedly and looked away from me.

"I always felt like writing an apology was like breaking up over text ya know, not quite what the situation deserved.

"Always? I guffawed. "You wrote a lot of apology letters before prison?

"Dear Aunt Sheryl, thank you for coming to my birthday party. Sorry I asked if were you pregnant. Thank you for the *Star Wars* Monopoly set.

"Please tell me that wasn't real.

"I would, but I try not to lie anymore. She was barren too, I actually made her cry.

"Oh my god, man, I said smiling harder than I thought I would today.

"No wonder I'm dying at thirty, huh?

"You found religion then?

"I know you think it's bullshit, but it's fuckin' real. I feel it, man.

"Not bullshit if it helps you, I disagreed.

"You still agnostic, though?

"I'm wrong a lot, I said with a shrug.

He nodded halfheartedly again, but he didn't turn away this time.

"Remember when Naomi tried to convince that Uber driver to do acid with her?

I laughed as we reenacted the story, happy that he changed the subject. We spent the rest of the half hour reminiscing about bullshit, laughing happily as if I wasn't the only one free to go. The congenial conversation made it easy, like old times.

I resisted the urge to yell at him about what a fucking socio-path he was and how I wanted to break the glass and beat his face into a mushy pulp. He probably knew. I'm sure he resisted the urge to tell me about all of his born again shit. I'm sure he knew.

What had been done couldn't be reversed and he was inca-pable of doing it again, so telling him off would've been cruel. Pointless. I was happy he was behind bars, it held my anxiety over what he'd do at bay. I knew this was cruel, but we can't control how we feel, only how we act. So I let that feeling sizzle in me, although I tried to reject the warmth it brought with it.

At the end we gave each other a slight fist bump across the glass and said our goodbyes. I promised to visit again before I couldn't and keep sending letters, especially the more spir-itual ones every few months. After that he was shuffled back into his hallway and I walked away from him.

I began my drive back to Flagstaff, my music reverberating through the aux. Instead of choosing a playlist I allowed my phone to pick from all of my ever liked songs. Flipping from music I enjoyed to songs I thought were "bangers as far back as middle school. An abundance of texts had been shot up on my display, from Luke, my sister, even a surprisingly kind one from my father. I ignored them all as my thoughts shifted from philosophical to the morbid, mundane to the existential. Two hours later I pulled into Annie's house, clutching the bag of fast food I had stopped for. I left my phone in my car as requested; the last time on my clock reading a little after eight. I rang her doorbell and waited hardly half a second before the door whipped open.

Naomi embraced me in a hug, shorter than I would have thought, and dragged me through the door. Annie was standing behind her, she had a forced smile and her eyes were puffy.

Annie was slightly taller than me with a thin build that was hidden by a thick hoodie. Her light purple hair was done up in a loose bun. Other than her hoodie she was only wearing jeans and indistinct glasses, her bare feet were immersed in the shag carpet that had supposedly come with the house. I always found that she did her best to blend in to the background when she wasn't working. Despite her efforts to disappear, Naomi had found her at a party and they'd been dating since before I got sober. I came up and gave her a hug which lasted much longer than Naomi's.

"You okay, Annie?

"Yeah, she replied unreassuringly.

"Wait, what was the time? Naomi asked.

"Naomi, Annie protested.

"Yeah, I thought we weren't doing that.

"Well, if you know, we might as well know. Otherwise it'll be awkward with you knowing more than us.

"I suppose, I replied. "It was a little after eight when I switched off the car.

"Okay, well I was born in Hawaii, so that means we got like seven hours left. Then I die. Now we can go completely off the grid, said Naomi.

"Okay, cool, I said.

"How are you feeling?

"I'm not ready, but I feel like I have closure. So I think that's all I can do, replied Naomi.

"I don't think anyone's ever ready, I replied.

"Well, in that case, I suppose I am ready.

"I'm not ready, Annie said.

I pulled her in for a small supportive hug as she went on.

"I can't believe God is doing this. She's such a cunt, said Annie.

I laughed and Naomi led us out of the hallway and into the living room. An especially slow song was playing from a speaker in the corner. There were two small blue couches facing the TV and an elegant coffee table in the middle with paraphernalia scattered on the edge. Annie's stripper pole was installed behind one of the couches; she told me previously she had to move the couch to practice.

"The microwave has been unplugged so you can't heat that up, said Annie

"That's fine, I said with a shrug, dropping my bag on the coffee table. "This song is a bit heavy.

"Yeah, I started the playlist when I was nineteen, called it 'Last Songs.' I felt I might as well play it. I switched my phone to airplane mode though; people kept trying to call me, said Naomi.

I shot a glance at Annie, but she wasn't there. She looked drained. "I mean, do you wanna take those?

"I took a lot, but I'm done. People have a lot they need to get off their chest, started to feel like I was a therapist. I just need to relax, she replied. "Want a beer? I got those non- alcoholic ones.

I took a seat on the couch. Annie sat on the other one, still on autopilot. Unsure of myself I reached onto the table and pulled a few buds out of the dispensary bag. I closed them in a small chrome grinder and began twisting, slight resistance at first until it slid like ice. I popped it open and dispersed it on a tray with a pun about getting high in Flagstaff on it. A simple classic. The smell wafted up and hit my nostrils. Good stoners will be able to tell you all about the strand from the smell, but I figured they were just high. Weed just smelled like weed.

Naomi plopped my beer down in front of me and laid down on the couch, her head in Annie's lap. She began poking Annie in the stomach.

"I thought you were California sober? I said looking at Naomi's drink.

"Well, I was, but I figure if I can't feel the hangover, I should drink like there is no tomorrow, she said raising her craft beer.

I raised my fake beer with her. "You still sober?

"Six months.

"Only six?

"Yeah, had a little relapse. When I woke up I was so scared that I cut up my driver's license so no one could sell me liquor. It took a couple weeks before my AA sponsor convinced me to get another one cause the last thing my paroled ass needs is to get arrested for driving without a license.

"You still get carded? Annie asked.

"Why didn't you tell me? Naomi interrupting Annie.

"Not really, and I just did.

Naomi rolled her eyes and looked back up at Annie. "Boys are the worst.

"Yeah, I can't believe you dated them.

"They're good for a few things.

Now it was Annie's turn to roll her eyes. It was also the first time she smiled tonight, it was a warm subtle smile, her lips barely turning upwards at the edge. I caught myself having my own bittersweet smile as I watched them. Naomi caught me third wheeling.

"So now what? I asked.

"We talk, Naomi replied. "TV, video games, all that stuff would just be a distraction. It's what we do to protect ourselves from boredom, but I doubt anyone is bored right now

"So, the economy is pretty weird, huh?

"Oh my god, Naomi said sitting up. "You're always so melodramatic and the one time I could use it, you get weird on me. How's your sister? Let's start there. You'd like her, she added to Annie.

"Good, graduated college with honors and is working through a med school in California. We talk every week now and I think she actually looks forward to it.

"What's her name? Annie asked.

"Reagan.

"That is a pretty name.

"Told you, Naomi said. "You think you're gonna stay sober for the next two years?

"I don't know, Naomi, I said. "My dad even agreed to go sober with me, it's only two more years, but it's still nice. I'm not gonna stop going to AA though.

"Okay, but how do you deal with the God aspect? asked Annie.

"Not well, that's why I go to secular AA meetings. They have those now, I answered.

"Do you want to drink now? Naomi asked.

"I always want a drink, Naomi, but I'd be damned if I forgot a single moment of tonight.

"Told you he was melodramatic, Naomi said to Annie.

"I've met him before, I know he's melodramatic.

"You gonna drink, like me, on your last day? Naomi asked me

"I'm actually planning on taking Molly.

"Oh, I should've done that, fuck beer.

I laughed and it got silent again.

"Naomi, are you scared?

"No, I'm not anymore. I'm extremely calm.

"How? I asked.

"People are usually calm before their death dates, their bodies go into shock. It's just a chemical reaction, but that's all we are: just chemical reactions.

"I love you, Naomi, I need you to know that, I said.

"I know, Danny. I love you, too.

I started crying. I started fucking sobbing. Tears dripping down my face as ugly moans escaped my lips. Naomi got up and sat next to me and wrapped her arms around me. Annie just watched and hugged a pillow. I felt so small. I felt so insignificant. I am so tired of being alive. The fucking rat race. We're just a bunch of worthless fucks scraping for meaning in a cold remorseless world. Holding onto each other as we dissipate. Searching for meaning where there is none. Fuck, I felt so small. I am so, so, so tired of being alive.

Eventually, I stopped crying.

We spent the next couple of hours talking. I told Naomi about my relationships and my one night stands. Annie told us her recipe for guacamole among other things. Naomi got drunk; I was tempted to do the same.

Then suddenly and slowly, Naomi stopped mid-sentence. Her favorite Lou Reed song, *A Perfect Day*, was playing. Her numbers turned blue on her wrist and she slumped into Annie who was holding her hand. Annie broke out in ugly sobs, sounds that would haunt me. I was empty by this point and I turned on my phone. I dialed 311, the non-emergency number, and told them that I had a dead body that needed picking up. It was three in the morning. Candles that burn twice as brightly die out twice as fast, and Naomi burned like a star.

I went over and hugged Naomi's body with Annie. I finally felt something that I was looking for all my life, peace. When the paramedics showed up I reluctantly got up. They pulled Annie away with a practiced stubbornness.

The paramedics came, the paramedics apologized, the paramedics left.

And again I felt so godforsaken, so perfectly alone.

Annie asked me to spend the night. I said I would as long as I could pour all of her alcohol down the drain. We poured a bourbon bottle worth $158 retail into a toilet. Then I slept in Naomi's place, not that I could ever replace her. God forbid I should try.

* * *

It was a little bit later and I was outside in the South Bronx. I was burning through a pack of American Spirits with Charlie as we stood outside a bar called Bar 47. I had taken the red-eye here the night before from Sky Harbor. It was a warm summer night and a cool breeze was blowing down the street. Charlie and I had been silent for a while. We both had been slugging nonalcoholics as we plugged away at the pool table.

"You going to Luke's wedding? I asked. "It's in Sedona.

"I mean I'm a cook living in the most expensive city in this hemisphere. I can't afford a plane ticket.

"I'll pick up your ticket if you come.

"Yeah?

"Yeah, now that Naomi is gone, I miss you even more, I said.

"Don't do that, just say you miss me. Don't compare me to anyone else.

"Sorry.

"It's okay.

We talked some more, we sat in silence some more, we smoked more cigarettes. It was nice and strangely lonely.

"How were Naomi's last moments?

"Good, I replied. "She was brave. I hope I will be brave, but I don't know if I have it in me.

"You'll be fine as long as you're sober, you know.

"I wake up every day craving a singular beer, Charlie. I don't know how much longer I can fight that, but on my last day I'm definitely having that fucking beer.

"You're stronger than you realize, but I'll only come to your funeral if you make it to the end. You OD again and you're dead to me.

"Can I OD on my last day?

"Sure, but that sounds like a horrible way to go.

"Fair enough.

We smoked in silence some more.

"I don't know if I'm strong enough, I said again.

"Then call me or Luke or Reagan. Just don't suffer alone.

"Okay, I said. "Charlie, I'm scared I'm gonna fuck everything up.

"You might, but I'll always be here for you. We'll do it together.

"That sounds nice, I said.

"Let's go back inside and play some pool.

We reentered the bar and everything was how it should be.

THE END

Author's Notes

"If I live too long I'm afraid I'll die. - *The Kinks*

"I'm a little messed up, it might be the drugs;
I'm a little fucked up, I might need a hug. - *Dune Rats*

"I wanna be a child climbing trees somewhere;
Breathing in the fresh outside air;
And before I knew this life was unkind. - *Zach Bryan*

My father once had an idea for a story. He's a neuro-radiologist so he sees people when they are on Death's doorstep. He told me that he thinks people would act differently if they knew the day they were going to die. He says that people who die in their twenties would party a lot and that that wasn't necessarily a bad choice. He said it would make a great story, but that he wasn't creative enough to write it, but that's where I come in.

I was obsessed with this idea and I wrote several short stories in college about this world, some of the characters actually found their way into this novel. I was a twenty-something-year-old kid and I was lost in the world, so it felt like the perfect vehicle to write about my grievances. I started taking the novel seriously when COVID happened. I was a stand-up comedian who couldn't perform anymore so I turned to writing. The rest is history.

I see myself and my friends in these characters. We also drank too much, had no real goals, and, for lack of a better term, were just trying to have a good time. Some of us spent time in rehab or the psych ward—personally I spent eighteen days in the psych ward—but we're all doing well now. We survived those days and are semi-functioning adults now. We were the original Joypunks.

I hope that this book fills you with optimism about the human condition. I hope you have a better understanding about those suffering from addiction. I hope you learned about the bohemians who are just searching for meaning in a meaningless world. May this book make you kinder, wiser, and fuller in your pursuit for human understanding. Thanks for taking the time to read it.

Sincerely,
Fletch (Jack) Fletcher

Acknowledgments

Firstly, I want to thank my father, without his initial idea I would've never been able to write this book. He is who I strive to be. I would like to thank my mother, the first person to read my book and tell me I should be published. Without her enthusiasm I would not have had the confidence to go forward. I would like to thank both of them for supporting me in my efforts to make a living with my creativity despite my father being a third-generation doctor.

I would like to thank my three brothers Sam, Hank, and Hayden. Sam, your intellectual curiosity makes you the most stimulating person I know to talk to. Henry, your constant drive to better yourself is something I look up to and helps me be better too. And Hayden, you helped remind me that even though both of us may not be doctors, engineers, lawyers, or firefighters, that we still are an important part of the family.

I would like to thank Kyle for getting a police warrant placed on our dorm Freshman year of college and for being my oldest, longest friend. I would also like to thank him for helping me contact his father, Ken, who convinced me to self-publish. I would like to thank Ken for introducing me to Marla. I would like to thank my book shepherd, Marla, for being with me every step of the way and making sure everything was perfect. I would like to thank my tireless editor, Christine, who made thousands of corrections on a two-hundred-page book. Without you, my writing would come across like the ramblings of a moron. I would like to thank Lauren of Pleasure Boat Studio for making phenomenal covers. We all secretly judge books by their covers and I'm grateful that she made mine. I would like to thank Jack from Pleasure Boat Studio for being the first in the industry to tell me to keep writing and for introducing me to Lauren.

Next, I want to thank Will, Kara, and Max. The three of you make my life easier and crazier and I'll forever want you three in my life. I want to thank Aidan, Jaiden, Johnny, Lane, Matt, Morgon, and Pappas for keeping me weird in high school. Without you guys I would be boring and blank. Special thanks to Magith who always gives me a shoulder to lean on and never judges me for a second. Thanks to Dhomas, Jess, Mary, Sam, and Topher for making my college years a wild time that I will never forget if only I could remember them in the first place. Thank you to Cara who is always down to drink with me no matter the occasion (and is funny as hell!). Thank you to Ash and Livy who convinced my grandmother not to read my book.

A thanks to the Psychiatric Unit of the Lincoln Hospital in the Bronx and the Banner Health Psychiatric Facility in Phoenix. Without the help of your Staff I would never have been able to recover. Thank you to Dr. Imig who has been with me through the worst of the worst. Thank you to my therapist Katrina who helped me find my feet again after New York. Thank you to Rose Cartwright for helping normalize OCD in your book *Pure*. You helped me feel less alone.

I would like to thank the staffs of the Eden Rooftop Bar, The Little Woody, The Spaghetti Tavern, and Babbo's for providing me employment and making work something to look forward too. Thank you for the comedians in the comedy scene in Tucson. You embraced an awkward nineteen year old and helped me feel at home despite being different. Thank you to Sarah

Harvard who was the only NYC comic to reach out after I left.

I would like to thank all the teachers and professors I've had over the years. Specific thanks to Mr. Fischer, Mrs. Blincoe, Miss Wehrspann, Mr. Smith, Mr. Donlan, MK, Mr. Unrein, and my countless writing professors at the University of Arizona.

Lastly, I want to thank everyone who read the first draft of my book and gave me notes to be better.

Thank you, all. I'm so grateful.

Included here are PREVIOUS RENDITIONS OF THE COVER, featuring a pine tree, prevalent in Arizona. Fletch Fletcher conceived this pine tree and the illustration of a hand holding a beer bottle. His idea was influenced by the style of modern Kurt Vonnegut covers. Covers created by Lauren Grosskopf, Pleasure Boat Studio, pleasureboatstudio.com

JOYPUNKS

Writing On the Wall

FLETCH FLETCHER

MONTE VISTA LOUNGE

JOYPUNKS

Writing On the Wall

MONTE
VISTA
LOUNGE

FLETCH
FLETCHER

JOYPUNKS

Writing On the Wall

FLETCH FLETCHER